The Black Storm

The Black Orchid Hotel

ROXANNE CARR

Black Lace novels are sexual fantasies.
In real life, make sure you practise safe sex.

First published in 1996 by
Black Lace
332 Ladbroke Grove
London
W10 5AH

Typeset by CentraCet Limited, Cambridge
Printed and bound by Mackays of Chatham PLC

ISBN 0 352 33060 0

For R.C.H.
Whose Encouragement
Meant So Much

Chapter One

The light filtering through the crack in the thick, red velvet curtains cast a jewel-like pattern on the soft, deep-pile carpet. Narrowing her eyes, Maggie watched it shimmer as she lay back on the couch, one full, soft-skinned breast enclosed in the heated mouth of the young man kneeling on the floor beside her.

He was naked, save for a pair of tight, black leather boxer shorts which left little to the imagination. His long, blond hair fell across his face, obscuring his features as he lathed diligently at her tumid nipple, rolling it on his tongue and suckling at it as if his life depended on it.

Meanwhile, further down the couch, an exotic-looking youth, half-African, half-Japanese, knelt between her legs and was lapping delicately at her tender labia. He had a deft, cat-like tongue and Maggie could feel herself responding to his efforts quite satisfactorily. His hands on her inner thighs were cool and soft skinned and he gave every appearance of enjoying himself.

1

Irritated by the heavy-tongued approach of the man at her breast, she tapped him hard on the shoulder, waving him away as he looked up at her with startled eyes. He rose awkwardly and his leather shorts pulled uncomfortably tight over his erection.

From the corner of her eye, Maggie saw the heavy oak door to the office open and Lena slipped discreetly through. Good – that meant she had been paying attention to the monitors in the inner office which showed what was taking place in this room.

Beckoning silently to the dismissed candidate, Lena ushered him through the door without any fuss and closed it quietly behind her.

Settling back comfortably, Maggie closed her eyes and pushed out her clitoris. The man at the end of the couch responded by increasing the speed of his tongue, pressing it firmly against the quivering bud as the first waves of orgasm passed through it.

Maggie gasped as the warmth spread rapidly outward – across her belly and along her arms and legs. Her hips bucked involuntarily and the young man who had extracted such a satisfying climax from her grasped her by the buttocks to keep her still. When at last the intensity became more subdued, he placed a small, thrilling kiss on the tip of the now softening nub of flesh before gently closing her legs and kissing her knees.

It was a strange, almost courtly gesture which had Maggie smiling approvingly at him as she sat up. Running her eyes over him as he stood quietly waiting for her to speak, she approved the broad, smooth-skinned sweep of his chest which tapered into a neat waist and a flat stomach. His skin was the colour of milky cocoa. It gleamed healthily in the subdued lighting, unmarred by the slightest hint of hair on his

2

chest or arms. Looking for telltale stubble, Maggie was pleased to find no sign that he had shaved off his body hair; he was naturally smooth and hairless. Had that state been artificial it would have been off-putting, as it was his lack of body hair gave him novelty value.

He was wearing jeans, simple 501's, clean, but well-worn. Remembering the other man's showy leather shorts, Maggie suppressed a shudder. 'What did you say your name was?' she asked him, reaching for her clipboard.

'I call myself Kokhi, ma'am – it's easier to say in English than my Japanese name.' He smiled, flashing white, even teeth at her and pushed his straight black hair out of his eyes.

'Well, Kokhi – come and sit down. Are you thirsty?'

'A cold drink would be good,' he replied.

Maggie went over to the repro fifties-style fridge in the corner of the office and took out two bottles of ice-cold cola. Levering off the caps, she eyed the young man sitting in the leather armchair opposite the couch.

He radiated a calm, restrained patience. She would have taken him for a submissive, but for the quiet competence of his love-making so far and a certain almost dangerous look in his light-brown eyes.

'You do realise, don't you,' she said as she handed him his drink, 'that waiting at table will be only a very small part of your duties here?'

'Oh yes, ma'am.' He smiled serenely at her and Maggie found herself smiling back.

'Call me Maggie,' she told him. 'I have to check. You see, we had one young man start with us when we first opened who genuinely believed he was to be a porter. He got quite a shock, I can tell you, when he realised he was expected to do far more than take a

3

client's case up to her room. How did you hear about us?'

'My sister stayed here before Christmas – I think she called herself Nadine?'

Maggie's eyes widened as she recalled the beautiful young woman who had wanted to explore the sapphic side of her sexuality. She herself had helped her to bring it out and Nadine had left a very satisfied customer.

'How is your sister?' she said softly, remembering.

Kokhi smiled. 'Very happy. She's settled in Paris with a modelling friend.'

'I see. She told you about her stay here?'

'Not in detail. But she was convinced that I would enjoy the work.'

Maggie regarded him thoughtfully. 'And you – do you think you would enjoy it? It can be quite exhausting.'

He smiled. 'The contracts are reasonably short, I understand?'

Maggie nodded. 'That's right. If we accept you, you must agree to undergo of a full medical screening. We expect you to live on the premises and will pay you to work in the kitchens until the results are through. That way you have little chance of coming into contact with the clients and you'll be so busy you won't have time to think about the period of enforced celibacy.'

Kokhi grimaced and took a swig of his drink. 'I'll pass the tests,' he said confidently. 'How long would you want me to sign up for?'

'Initially, three months. If after that time you want to stay longer, we would extend the contract for a further six months.'

'And then?'

'Then we insist you have a break. Our rules are very strict – no physical contact between members of staff, unless as part of an entertainment for the guests. And no relationships outside the hotel. We have to be very careful. Obviously, no one is expected to do anything that they find repulsive, but we do expect our staff to be game for most forms of sexual play. Do you think you could hack it?'

Kokhi put down his empty cola bottle and looked back at her steadily. 'I think so.'

Maggie smiled slowly at him. 'Very well, All that's left for me to do now is check you can use all your God-given talents.'

She watched through narrowed eyes as Kokhi rose without a word and began to unbutton his jeans. He was quick on the uptake – another point in his favour. To her surprise Maggie found she was holding her breath as she realised he wasn't wearing underwear. As elsewhere on his body, the hair at his groin was sparse, but very black and silky looking. As he pushed the heavy fabric down his legs, his penis sprang free, and Maggie assessed him critically.

It was long and slender, the brown skin very smooth, the veins almost invisible. His foreskin had retracted to reveal the velvety, purplish bulb, the end of which was already glistening with the clear fluid of pre-emission. Beneath, his scrotum was full and ripe, lightly furred with short black hair.

Once he was naked, Kokhi stood in front of her for a moment, as if unsure whether he was expected to make the next move. Sensing his dilemma, Maggie handed him a condom from the laquer jewel box she kept on the coffee table. Then she opened the red silk robe she had fastened round her and held out her arms to him.

5

To her delight, he was restrained as he covered her body with his; seeing his arousal she had half expected him to try to enter her straightaway. Instead, he manoeuvred himself so that he could run his penis up and down over her shaven mons, indirectly stimulating her clitoris which had slipped quietly back beneath its protective hood.

Maggie's arms snaked up around his neck and she allowed her thighs to fall softly open so that his cock-head was nudging the moist folds of her labia. Drawing back slightly, Kokhi drew back slightly, and let his eyes scan her features, gauging the level of her desire. Seeing her readiness, he entered her with one swift, sure stroke, then lay, completely still, his engorged penis resting inside her.

He was very slender, but not too skinny. Running her palms over his shoulders and back, Maggie could feel the wiry strength of him and guessed that he took good care of his body. He clearly had plenty of experience with women and took pleasure in ensuring his partner achieved satisfaction, giving quite selflessly until he was sure he had done enough. In essence, he was an ideal candidate and Maggie was sure that he would fit in very well at the Black Orchid Hotel.

While these objective assessments were running through her mind, a subtler, more physical process was taking place deep in her womb. She sighed as Kokhi began to move inside her, his strokes slow and sure, almost leisurely, as he coaxed her back to the peak of arousal.

His smooth, cocoa-coloured skin gradually became slick beneath her palms as his tempo increased. The room would have been completely silent but for the sound coming from Kokhi as he approached his climax and issued a long, low gasp. Maggie wriggled her hips slightly so that he was stimulating her recently sated flesh once again and quickly joined him in a short, sharp climax, the intensity of which made her head swim.

It was a minute or two before he withdrew from her, dropping a kiss on her cheek as he did so.

'So beautiful,' he murmured and Maggie smiled. That was exactly what many of their clients wanted to hear after they had been thoroughly serviced by the staff.

'Thank you, Kokhi,' she said, her voice faintly husky, losing its objective, professional edge, as they tidied themselves. 'Subject to the tests we spoke of, how soon could you start?'

He grinned, his face lighting up as he realised he'd passed the interview. 'Actually I handed in the keys to my flat before I left, so I'd be happy to stay from now on, if that would suit you.'

Maggie raised her eyebrows. 'You were very confident.'

Kokhi shrugged self-deprecatingly. 'My sister told me about you. I knew if you liked her, there was a fair chance that you would like me too.'

Hiding a smile, Maggie tried to look stern, and failed. 'It's not important that I should like you, Kokhi. The customer is the one who's always right. Don't ever forget that.'

'I won't, ma'am.'

'Good. Go and see Lena – she'll sort you out a room and book you an appointment with the doctor.'

She waited until he had left before going through to the sumptuous bathroom attached to her office for a shower. She felt exhausted, not just physically, but emotionally too. She had interviewed five potential members of staff today, three male, two female, and of those five only two had measured up. Kokhi and a petite blonde called Susie who made no secret of the fact that she enjoyed every kind of sexual encounter, just so long as it involved her own ritualised humiliation.

The others – Well! She grimaced as the warm water streamed over her face and down the front of her body. They all left a great deal to be desired. The trouble with so many of the people who heard about the hotel, or knew about the original Black Orchid Club, was that they assumed the staff were primarily there for their own satisfaction. Only those who truly liked women, who genuinely enjoyed giving rather than receiving pleasure, were suitable for the highly specialised work she had on offer.

A great many of the more unsuitable applicants were weeded out before interview stage by a carefully worded questionnaire. But, because of the very intimate nature of the work, the only way to be absolutely sure was to invite likely-looking candidates for a personal interview.

Maggie had tried delegating the task of interviewing, but the experiment had been a disaster. No one else had her experience in the field, no one else had her instinct for what made a good 'waiter'.

Turning off the shower, she sighed heavily, then dried herself on a thick white towel and applied a thin layer of talcum powder all over. After slipping into underwear and a cream silk pyjama suit, she renewed her make-up – smoky-grey eye shadow and bright-red lipstick – and brushed out her long, dark hair.

Lena was waiting for her when she emerged from the bathroom and Maggie smiled. She was very fond of the cheerful redhead who worked with her as a secretary and gopher. Lena had her finger on the pulse of the goings-on at the hotel and often acted as Maggie's unofficial eyes and ears.

She was not here now, though, to report on problems brewing in the gym or the dining room. She had come to tell Maggie that she had a visitor.

'Antony's here!' Maggie exclaimed, all her former weariness forgotten.

'I put him in the library so that you'd have time to finish in here,' Lena said, leaning forward to pick a stray hair off Maggie's lapel. 'I'll see to the dinner period this evening, shall I?'

'Oh would you, Lena? You're a gem. It's been so long since I saw Antony, I'd be glad to forget the routine, just for one evening.'

'No problem,' Lena grinned. 'Have fun.'

Maggie gave her a quick hug before hurriedly leaving the room to find Antony. Lena stared after her, struggling with the jealousy that had reared its ugly head the moment Antony had appeared in reception.

Antony seemed engrossed in a book that he had picked off the shelves as Maggie entered the library and she had a few minutes to study him before he was aware of her presence. His back was to the door; his shoulders sloping slightly as he held the book by the window to catch the light. His thick, gold-blond hair was slightly longer than usual, curling onto the collar of the denim shirt he was wearing tucked into his jeans. Maggie felt a surge of affection rock her at the unexpected sight of him.

'Antony.'

He turned and she was gratified to see his frank grey eyes light up with delight as he saw her.

'Maggie,' he said, abandoning the book on the side table and holding out his arms to her.

She was across the room in half-a-dozen strides and was immediately enveloped in his all-encompassing embrace.

'Oh Antony – it's so good to see you.' She smiled up at him, concerned to see the faint lines of strain around his eyes. 'Why didn't you let me know you were coming?'

'Spur of the moment thing. Can you manage to get away? It's a beautiful afternoon, I thought we might take a walk as far as the estuary and back.'

'It's already arranged. Would you like a quick look round first – see how your investment is coming along?'

'Later, perhaps. Let's take advantage of the sunshine now. I'll just put this back on the shelf. You've added some books to your collection since I was last here, I see.'

Maggie glowed with pride. Her library of erotica was growing fast and was already attracting attention from other serious collectors.

'I think it's important to gather together more contemporary authors as well as the old stalwarts, don't you? After all, some of these might well become the classics of tomorrow.'

'Absolutely.' He smiled at her and held out his hand.

They strolled together, hand in hand, through the wide-flung French doors leading from the library, and down the stone steps which led to the lawn. At the far side of the gentle incline was a vast bank of rhododendron bushes, just coming into bloom. Beyond, the silver sparkle of the Atlantic was visible over the cliff.

'So – how's it going?' Antony said when they had walked in companionable silence for several minutes.

'Well, I spoke to Sally Warner the other day, and she reckons that, considering we've only been in business for eight months, the books are looking pretty healthy. But you must know that, Antony. I can't believe that you haven't been in touch with her yourself.'

'You know me too well. No, I mean how are you coping?'

Maggie bit her lip and paused to cup a rhododendron bud in her palm. The deep purple flower was pushing its way inexorably through the tightly furled greenery, ready to burst into bloom.

'I don't know, Tony,' she mused, not thinking to tell him anything but the truth. 'I feel so restless these days. I get so *bored* to be honest.'

'Oh dear,' Antony linked his arm through hers and they walked through the gap in the bushes and onto the path which led to the cliff top walk. 'Yours isn't the kind of work you can do well if your heart's not in it. Is it anything specific?'

Maggie thought of the interviews she had conducted that morning and sighed. 'Half the trouble is that you just can't get the staff these days.' She laughed and extricated her arm from Antony's so that she could stretch out her shoulders. 'Don't take any notice of me – I'll revive again, no doubt. I'm probably just feeling a bit jaded, that's all.'

'Hmm.' Antony regarded her with wry amusement. 'I'll put the word out at the Club that you're recruiting again – there are one or two trainers whose contracts are up for renewal who might fancy a change of scene. Meanwhile what you need, my girl, is a little diversion.'

11

Maggie laughed, linking arms with him again as they turned left and began to walk along the cliff top towards the path which led down to the estuary, a mile away.

'I'd appreciate it if you could shunt a few men my way – at least they're already trained and know what to expect. Anyway, enough about me. Have you heard from Alexander lately?'

She could have bitten out her tongue when she saw the way Antony's handsome face clouded over. He had found it difficult when Alexander left for California six months before to set up a new venture with his father, Tourell. Both Antony and Maggie could have gone with them, but they had chosen to cling to what little independence there was left to them, Antony staying with the health club while she was busy setting up the fledgling hotel.

'Do you regret not going?' she asked, gently now.

Antony gazed out across the sea, his eyes misty. 'They needed the time alone together, to sort things out. I would have come between them.'

'He'll be back before too long,' Maggie said after a few moments, 'you'll see.'

Antony smiled bravely at her. 'Of course he will. He'd never find anyone else to put up with him the way I do.'

They carried on walking, each wrapped up in their own thoughts. Maggie reflected on Antony and Alexander's complex relationship, wondering if it would endure. Certainly, the balance of power had seemed to shift in the time that she had known them, and Alexander had, at last, admitted his deep and abiding love for the man walking at her side. In many ways they were as close as any married couple, though each was unfaithful to the other as a matter of course at the Black Orchid Club. Unlike Antony, though, Alex had never been able to resist casting his net wider than the club, and it was common for him to disappear for days on end every few months.

This time, though, it was different. Alexander had gone away to repair his relationship with his father and for the first time since she had known them, he was not putting Antony first. This development clearly hurt, even though Antony was the one who had done all he could to bring Alexander and Tourell together, knowing how much the estrangement had upset Alex.

Remembering the part she had played in their reconciliation still made her heart ache. Her time with Tourell had been so short; so many things had been left unresolved – had she done the right thing by walking out on him?

Maggie jumped out of her skin as, from out of nowhere, it seemed, a motorbike roared past them on the narrow path, wrenching her rudely from her reverie and forcing both of them dangerously close to the cliff edge.

'Maniac,' she screamed at the retreating biker, shaking uncontrollably as Antony grabbed her arm.

'Steady, Maggie. God, you're shaking like a leaf.'

'He could have killed us.'

'He was pretty close, yes, but don't forget that he saw us before we saw him. He would have steered round us.'

'Oh Antony,' Maggie buried her face momentarily in his chest, acknowledging how the biker had shaken her. 'How come you're always so bloody reasonable?'

They laughed and quickened their pace, determined to reach the estuary before turning back.

The mouth of the river was home to several houseboats which bobbed peacefully on the Cornish tide. Maggie knew every one by sight since she often took this route to the village where they bought most of their supplies. To her surprise, this time there was a new boat moored at the side of the river. And standing outside it was a shiny black motorbike.

Antony spotted it at the same time as her. 'Now Maggie . . .'

She ignored him and broke into a run, the memory of the fright she had been given still fresh in her mind.

'Hey – you in there,' she shouted as she reached the boat.

There was a movement on the inside, then the door was filled by six-foot-two of leather-jacketed muscle. Maggie took in the long black hair and aggressive stance and her mouth tightened. Hard blue eyes travelled over her silk pyjama suit, incongruous on the river bank, and firm lips twitched in amusement as she bristled visibly.

'Yeah?'

'You're the maniac who nearly ran us down just now on the cliff path. Are you blind or something?'

The man quirked an eyebrow and Maggie noticed, irrelevantly, that a small scar divided one brow neatly into two.

'Did the bike splash you?' he drawled in a lazy, West Country burr.

Maggie put her hands on her hips and thrust out her chin. 'No it didn't splash me. But it damn well nearly drove me off the cliff. The least you could do is apologise.'

She was vaguely aware that Antony had caught up with her and was waiting patiently some yards away for her to finish venting her spleen on the hapless biker.

'Apologise? Lady, you can crawl up your own arse.'

Maggie's jaw dropped as he turned away dismissively. Without thinking, she jumped onto the deck of the boat and grabbed him by the shoulder, intending to spin him round to face her. She didn't expect him to whirl round, knocking her off balance so that, instead of threatening him, she was forced to grab his lapels to stop herself from toppling over into the water.

'Oh!'

The pungent smell of axle grease and old leather filled her nostrils and for a moment she felt dizzy. The man's face was close to hers – too close – she could see every pore on his face, feel the pure, animal heat emanating from his body. He had several day's beard growth on his jaw and for one, extraordinarily lucid second, Maggie had a vivid image of it rasping over her naked skin.

Her eyes widened and something flashed across the hard, blue surface of his eyes. Incredibly, Maggie felt the unmistakable, liquid response of arousal flood through her and she clung to him, aware that his body too had responded to her nearness. The hard arms which held her tensed, then he thrust her from him roughly, a look of such disgust passing over his features that she felt shaken.

'You're trespassing, lady,' he grated, his voice harsh.

Maggie scrambled inelegantly on to the bank, anxious to put a safe distance between them. Once safely on the bank, she turned, her eyes blazing. 'Just watch where you're going in future,' she said, angry at the audible quaver in her voice.

'You too,' he responded coldly.

Gathering her dignity about her, Maggie walked

15

back to join Antony, conscious of the biker's eyes boring into her back as she moved away.

'Come on Antony – let's head back,' she said between her teeth.

Glancing towards the houseboat, Antony took her arm and walked with her back the way they had come. 'Maybe that's your answer, Maggie,' he said after a few minutes.

'My answer?' Maggie's mind had been far away, still on the deck of the houseboat, saying all the clever, biting things she should have said to that uncouth lout, but didn't.

'Yes.' He tilted his head back towards the estuary. 'A bit of rough would be a change for you.'

'A bit of – Antony! If you think I was the slightest bit attracted to that – that *animal*, then you're out of your mind.'

Maggie wrenched herself out of his grasp and stormed ahead, cheeks flaming as she recalled the swift, unwanted flare of arousal she had felt when the man had held her on the boat. A bit of rough indeed – Antony had to be kidding.

'Come on,' she shouted over her shoulder as she saw that he was lagging behind. 'I presume you're staying for tonight's party?'

'Could do.' He was smiling, obviously amused by her reaction to his suggestion. 'What's happening?'

Maggie shrugged. 'A floor show, a bit of music. Mass copulation – you know the form.'

Antony laughed. 'Sounds like my kind of evening. Let's get back and we'll squeeze in that tour before the party starts.'

Maggie nodded and followed him, resisting the urge to look behind her to see if she was still being watched by those hard, blue eyes.

Chapter Two

*A*ntony watched Maggie's face carefully as she told him about the latest developments at the hotel. In spite of what she had said about becoming jaded, he could see her enthusiasm was still intact as she talked about their joint venture.

'We're booked solidly for the next three weeks and have already begun to take reservations for as far away as next June,' she was telling him now, her lovely face flushed with pleasure as she contemplated their success.

'I still think that your primary strength will lie in the last-minute, impulse bookings,' he said. 'After all, self-indulgence is what this place is all about, and what could be more self-indulgent than an unplanned weekend acting out one's most secret fantasies?'

He waggled his eyebrows at her and Maggie laughed.

'You love it, don't you, Antony? All this,' she said, sweeping her arm in an arc to take in the enormous, luxurious pool with its impossibly blue water fringed by exotic plants. 'You had a dream when you started up the Black Orchid Club, and it's never left you. You've never lost the belief that drives you on, have you?'

Antony stared at her, aware that, as she spoke, a wave of affection for her had washed over him, taking him by surprise. Impulsively, he reached out and cupped her face. Maggie looked surprised, but she didn't move, merely gazing quizzically at him as he caressed the soft swell of her cheek with his thumb.

'What belief is that, Maggie?' he asked her, his voice low. He saw that she swallowed before she answered, as if she had caught his mood and shared his feelings.

'The belief that all women are beautiful . . .'

'In their own way,' he finished for her when she trailed off.

Maggie smiled and, turning her head, pressed her lips into his palm. The small, wet kiss sent little strobes of electricity rushing along his arm.

'And yet the love of your life is another man,' she said, something colouring her tone which sounded to Antony suprisingly like regret. Dropping his hand, he put his arm lightly around Maggie's shoulders and strolled with her out of the pool room towards the lounge.

'I don't see men and women as separate categories,' he offered. 'I just see people. Everyone is different, unique – *interesting* to me.'

'As I was?'

He smiled, remembering the uptight strong executive who, once introduced to the many pleasures it had to offer, had embraced the ethos of the club with such enthusiasm. 'Ah,' he said, turning to kiss her hair, 'you were different. Special. I knew you wouldn't be content with mere membership for long. I knew, from the very first moment I saw you – '

'Maggie, I'm sorry to interrupt, but the chef needs to speak with you.'

They both turned as Lena approached them. She wore a harried, overworked expression that Antony recognised and sympathised with. He smiled at the woman and was surprised by the open hostility in her vivid green eyes.

'I've taken up quite enough of your time,' he told Maggie as she turned apologetically to him. 'It's not as if you knew I was coming. Lena has already allocated a room for me – I could do with some sleep. Maybe we can enjoy the show together later?'

Giving him a grateful smile, Maggie squeezed both his hands and nodded. 'Yes – I'll see to it that we have a table. See you later.'

Antony thrust his hands into his pockets and watched as Maggie walked swiftly away with Lena. The redhead hurried ahead to open the door for her, touching her elbow briefly as she passed, as if guiding her through. Antony looked thoughtful as the doors closed behind them and he was left alone in the plush silence of the hallway.

Maggie worried him. During their last telephone conversation she had seemed edgy, restless and what she had said today about being jaded underscored his reading of the situation. He thought of the biker and her almost primaeval reaction to him and he smiled. If she had only known how clearly her feelings were written on her face, Maggie would have been mortified. Even so, he had only been teasing her when he had suggested she might be yearning for rough trade. Here she was protected, in control. He didn't like the thought of her striking up a liaison with someone

19

outside the organisation. Certainly not with someone as potentially unpredictable as the biker.

No, he concluded, making his way to his room, Lena was a much better bet to assuage Maggie's sudden restlessness. If he had correctly interpreted the woman's hostility towards him as jealousy, and was not mistaken about her body language, then Lena was in love with Maggie. Maggie herself didn't seem to have recognised it yet, but Antony had no doubt that she would not be averse to the idea to a love affair with the beautiful redhead. After all, that kind of adoration was a powerful aphrodisiac.

Resolving to do all he could to encourage her along that path rather than towards the itinerant biker on the estuary, Antony promised himself a quiet hour in his room before the entertainment to come.

Lena watched as Maggie dealt with the temperamental chef with her usual charm and firmness.

'How do you do it?' she asked admiringly as they left the steamy kitchens and made one last check of the main entertainment room.

Maggie rolled her eyes at her. 'God knows! Between you and me, Lena, I don't think I'm really cut out for this kind of thing.'

'Nonsense. I don't know anyone who could run this hotel the way you do. Maggie – you *are* the Black Orchid Hotel!'

Catching her employer's startled glance, Lena realised she'd been a little too effusive with her praise. Far too passionate. Forcing a rueful smile, she drew Maggie's attention to the fresh flower arrangements on each table and at the edge of the stage.

'They're beautiful, Lena,' Maggie said, pensively eyeing the blood-red roses and dramatic foliage. 'You have a knack for knowing exactly what will please our clients.'

Happily savouring Maggie's approval, Lena followed her back to reception.

'Right,' Maggie said briskly, 'have you identified which of the guests would be most suitable to take part in the floor show tonight?'

Lena opened a drawer and took out a seating plan. 'I've put Eleanor Barrington here,' she said, pointing to a table to one side of the stage.

Picturing the elegant, controlled businesswoman in her mind's eye, Maggie raised her eyebrows, though she said nothing, waiting for Lena to continue.

'Then on this side, Sara Lawson will be with Marc and Jason. Sara isn't likely to refuse to get up with those two – apparently she's been closeted in her room with them ever since she arrived.'

Catching a note of disapproval in her secretary's voice, Maggie frowned. 'Yes, I can see that Sara is a good choice,' she said impatiently, 'but where does Eleanor fit in?'

'Ah,' Lena smiled, holding up her forefinger to stop Maggie from continuing. 'George has been waiting on Eleanor, and he is convinced she'd welcome the chance to get it on with another woman – given the right push.'

Maggie didn't question whether the 'right push', as Lena put it, might not be a very public stage in the middle of a hotel ballroom. In her experience erotic submission very often occurred in the most unlikely of locations, during the most bizarre situations, so she merely nodded, smothering a yawn with the back of her hand.

'Very well. You know, I'm wiped out after the

21

interviews this morning – I think I'll have a couple of hours rest. Can you cope here?'

'Of course – everything is under control. Would you like me to run your bath for you?' Lena was conscious that she was holding her breath as she waited for Maggie's reply.

'That would be nice. Come to think of it, so would one of those wonderful shoulder massages you've been perfecting,' she added with a mischievous twinkle in her eye.

Lena felt her cheeks grow warm and she dropped her eyes. Had Maggie guessed how desperate she was to get close to her? Glancing at her quickly from beneath her lashes, she saw that her employer was putting the seating plan away, apparently unconcerned, and she relaxed.

Following Maggie up the narrow staircase which led to the staff quarters, Lena feasted her eyes on the gentle swing of her hips, focusing on the way the silky material of her pyjama suit clung to the firm, rounded globes of her buttocks. She swallowed a sigh. It shouldn't be difficult, given the nature of the hotel, to make her feelings known. After all, she knew that Maggie quite happily swung both ways and enjoyed making love to both men and women.

That was probably the problem, Lena conceded to herself as they reached Maggie's suite. She didn't want to be just another notch on her employer's bedpost. What she felt for Maggie was special. She knew it could be good between them – lasting. The question was how she was going to make Maggie see her as more than her indispensable, hard-working right-hand woman. How could she make her see her as a *woman* at all?

Maggie's living room-cum-bedroom was decorated

in a calm, uncluttered style which Lena admired, though did not particularly like. The walls were painted cream, the carpet was an unfussy, caramel, twist pile. On one wall there were twin sash windows which looked across the gardens to the woodland which bordered the grounds of the hotel. In the distance the sea could be seen, a thin sliver of sapphire-blue drawing a line beneath the sky.

Closing the plain, gold-coloured silk curtains, Lena crossed the room into the small gold and cream, mirrored ensuite bathroom and turned on the bath taps. Back in the bedroom, she watched as Maggie rummaged through the wardrobes which covered the entire wall on either side of the bathroom door.

Lena nodded when Maggie held up a short, ruby-red evening dress for her approval. 'That suits you, Maggie,' she said. 'wear it with those really high stilettoes that were sent from America.'

Lena saw how Maggie's hand faltered as she reached for the sandals and felt jealousy stab her through the heart. Of course – they were from *him*. Alexander – the lover she had heard so much about but had never met. She had no reason to hate him as she did, she acknowledged silently, but she hated the way the mere mention of his name, the slightest reminder of him, gave Maggie that faraway look in her eye that excluded Lena so totally. And this time she was the one who had inadvertently brought him to mind, dammit! 'Bath's ready,' she said brightly to distract her.

Maggie lay her outfit ready on the bed and, shrugging off her clothes, walked naked into the bathroom, apparently totally oblivious to Lena's lustful eyes following her every move.

* * *

23

Maggie lay back in the warm, jasmine-fragranced water and closed her eyes.

'Mmm, Lena, this is bliss,' she breathed.

The other woman came up behind her and began to knead the tight muscles in her neck and shoulders with warm, sure fingers. Maggie sighed. It crossed her mind that this was assistance above and beyond the call of duty, but she did not examine the thought. Lena was a gem, pure and simple, and she made a mental note to make sure that her end-of-year bonus reflected that.

After Lena had gone, Maggie topped up the bath water in preparation for a serious soak. Her thoughts turned to Antony and his unexpected visit. She was glad to see him, but knew that there was likely to be some purpose to his arrival. She shrugged. What did it matter? So long as he found everything in order and enjoyed the programme tonight, what could possibly worry him?

When the water began to cool, Maggie climbed out of the bath, towelled herself dry, and massaged fragrant oil into her skin before padding naked back through to the bedroom. The skimpy red dress glided over her supple skin, clinging to every curve and dip so that to wear underwear would have been impossible. Running her hands from her breasts to her thighs to smooth the material, Maggie surveyed herself critically in the floor-to-ceiling mirrors.

The hotel had a gym to equal the one at the Black Orchid Club, so she continued to work out diligently at least four times a week. It showed; her long legs were subtly sculpted, her buttocks, high and taut. There wasn't an inch of spare flesh around her trim waist and her breasts were firm and well supported, giving every appearance of uplift even without the

24

help of a bra. Though her shoulders were covered by the red dress, her arms were bare and she was pleased to see that there was no discernible sign of the lithe, well-honed musculature slackening – they resembled the carefully crafted arms of a marble statue.

Well-pleased with her appearance, Maggie slipped her tanned feet into the spindly sandals Alexander had sent her from America. The ridiculously high heels strained the muscles in her calves and threw her feet into an unnatural position, elongating the arches and making her walk almost exclusively on the ball of her foot. Even standing in the shoes made her breath catch in her throat and her pulse flutter. They made her think of sex. Immediately, she felt the heat trickle up her legs, through her calves, her knees, sweeping up her thighs which began to tremble. Slowly, on shaky legs, she walked over to the mirror and stood in front of it.

In the past, whenever Alexander had wanted her to follow his, very specific, instructions, he had always laid out extraordinarily high heels for her to wear. Probably because her movements were so restricted in them, they made her feel helpless, vulnerable in a way that she never normally felt in everyday life. Alexander understood instinctively that, as a precursor to submission, the shoes played a crucial role.

There was an ocean between them now, they were on separate continents. Yet now, like a well-trained marionette, she had become aroused by the mere act of slipping into the shoes he had sent her. All she had to do was slip her fingers under her skirt . . .

Maggie stared at her reflection as she exposed the pink-skinned, shaven mound of her mons. Her labia were already swollen, protruding slightly from her outer lips – the smooth, darker-pink flesh glistening with the evidence of her arousal. Her fingertips described small, concentric circles on her inner thighs as she edged them towards the sensitive vulval flesh.

Breathing faster, Maggie caressed her breasts through the thin fabric of her dress, watching as her nipples sprang to life beneath her fingers, two hard, perfect circles pressing against the fabric. She touched herself, oh-so gently, at the point where her labia met. A sharp, zinging sensation shot through her, making her gasp.

Slowly, watching herself intently in the mirror, Maggie began to stroke the delicate folds of flesh, gradually opening them and slipping her fingers into the inner channels. Bending slightly at the knees, she parted her moisture-slick outer labia to reveal the shiny folds of flesh within which opened to her gaze like the petals of a flower.

In the mirror, she could see the shadowed channel into her body below her urethra, and above that could see the hard little pip of her clitoris expanding beneath its protective hood of flesh.

She felt hot, moving her fingertips faster and faster across the slippery skin. Her legs strained to keep her balance and her mouth slackened as she felt the sensations building, building in the pit of her stomach.

Visions of Alexander swam before her eyes. Beautiful, golden, cruel Alexander who kept both her and Antony, who loved him, dangling at his whim. How she missed him! Missed his clever fingers, his knowing tongue, his unpredictable, heartless streak. Life with Alexander had never been dull, sex never less than sensational.

Maggie frowned as, in her mind's eye, a darker, coarser image gradually superimposed itself over

Alexander's golden image. Cool, knowing, blue eyes were obliterated by a hard, mocking, denser-blue gaze. Maggie moaned a soft denial as she recognised the biker. She didn't want the thought of him to arouse her – her climax belonged to Alex, not to a nameless stranger.

It was too late to control it, too late to bring her recalcitrant memory under control. Though the rational part of her denied it, Maggie knew that she found the very thought of being with the biker powerfully exciting. He was an unknown entity, erotic, unpredictable, *dangerous*.

She came, gasping and shuddering, her fingers coated with the thick honey-juice of her body, her breasts aching for more than her own gentle caress. Swallowing hard, Maggie regarded her flushed face and over-bright eyes in the mirror and grimaced. It might have been the biker's face that swum before her eyes, she thought defiantly, but it was the thought of Alexander that had aroused her in the first place. Always Alex.

'Damn you, Alexander – you've spoilt me for anybody else,' she said, her voice low and filled with emotion.

Then she smiled, stretching like a cat and revelling in the warm glow which spread through her body. Straightening, she went through to the bathroom and tidied herself, gathering her composure. She had more reason to thank Alexander than to damn him. Without his guidance she would never have found herself doing a job which, though admittedly it had begun to pall of late, was generally the job of her dreams. A career devoted to divining the innermost fantasies of her clients, to helping other women discover their true sexual potential.

There was nothing more satisfying to her than seeing a woman who had arrived tense and unsure of herself slowly sloughing off her inhibitions, experimenting with her own sexuality. Hugging the exciting discovery to herself as she left after her stay, knowing that now everything was open to her.

No, Maggie smiled, she would not let her own feelings jeopardise her personal crusade. And tonight there was someone here who shared her dreams – she would enjoy Antony's company, as always.

Heartened, Maggie ran a brush through her long, dark hair and went downstairs to join her guests.

Antony was waiting for her at a small, round table set discreetly towards the back of the room, in a position where Maggie could keep an eye on her guests and staff whilst still enjoying the show herself. There was a vase of fading red roses in the centre of the table and a Martini waiting at the empty place.

'Hi.' She smiled at him, putting her hands in his as he rose to greet her.

At six-three, Antony generally towered over everyone else and the dark fabric of his dinner jacket showed off his physique to its best advantage. He looked older now than when she had first met him; the lines scoring his tanned face from nose to mouth and across his forehead were deeper, but it suited him, added *gravitas* to his already impressive appearance.

Antony was scrutinising her no less closely and Maggie wondered what he was thinking. The subdued lighting softened the bright blond of his hair to the colour of wheat and shadowed his expression so she had no way of guessing.

'I took the liberty of ordering for you,' he said as

they took their seats. 'Rainbow trout with new potatoes and salad.'

'Lovely,' she assured him, turning her attention to her guests.

The room was filling up steadily ready for the show. There were fourteen women staying at present and each one who wished it was escorted by a 'waiter', male or female. Each of the men, hand-picked by Maggie, was wearing formal evening dress like Antony. The female staff were each given a wardrobe of three 'dressy' outfits for these occasions.

Where there had been more than one woman requesting the company of a particular attendant, they had been accommodated on larger tables. Maggie caught the eye of one particularly popular young man, a devil-may-care Irishman called Derry, and gave him a sympathetic smile. He was battling manfully to divide his attention between three different women, all of whom had taken a strong fancy to him. Maggie made a mental note to arrange for reinforcements to be sent to help out should he disappear with the full coterie.

Antony, who missed nothing, touched Maggie's elbow.

'Who's that?'

'His name's Derry – short for Derek, I think.'

'Doesn't have the same ring to it,' Antony said with a grin.

'Right. He's only been with us for two months, but already I've had to take him off duty twice to give him a breather.'

'What makes him so popular?'

Maggie grinned. 'Because, my love, he's hung like the proverbial donkey.' She laughed as she recognised

29

the spark of interest in Antony's eyes. 'Strictly a ladies' man, I'm afraid.'

Antony's face registered disappointment, and he shrugged. 'Oh well. Looks like we're about to start.'

Movement behind the cloth backdrop to the stage preceded a sudden blast of loud music. Maggie sipped her Martini and watched as The Body Beautiful – six young men in policemen's uniform – burst onto the stage and began to dance.

The Body Beautiful were a regular act at the Black Orchid Hotel. Maggie had first encountered them at the club when their lead dancer was a young, arrogant gigolo called Electric Blue. She smiled to herself as she recalled her encounter with that particular performer on the cold linoleum of his dressing room floor between sets.

She'd watched him dance and gyrate on the raised podium in the middle of the room, surrounded by wildly cheering women, and then followed him when he'd finished. She'd bound his wrists with his own hair and played with the intriguing arrangement of gold chains which connected his nipples to his beautiful cock.

Unfortunately, Electric Blue was no longer a part of the troupe. Which was just as well, Maggie conceded, since she had quite enough on her hands at present. Sensing that Antony was watching her, she smiled at him, reaching across the table to cover his hand with hers.

'How are you coping with being in charge of your own destiny now that Alexander has gone?' she asked him, leaning forward so that he could hear her over the din.

Antony raised an eyebrow at her. 'Do you think physical distance makes a difference?'

Maggie considered. Once she, like Antony, had willingly submitted to Alexander's authority. He had held the key to her every sexual response, was the driving force behind every impulse. With a rueful *moue* she thought of how she had masturbated earlier, turned on by the mere act of slipping into the shoes he had sent her.

'No. Will we ever be free, do you think?'

'Do you want to be?'

Antony was watching her closely and Maggie guessed that her response to his question would be remembered, and possibly relayed to Alex. Nevertheless, she was being honest when she replied, 'No. Sometimes I think I want to be. But when it comes down to it, I would miss his presence in my head.'

Smiling, Antony lifted her hand to his lips and pressed them against her knuckles. 'Have you any idea how much I love you?' he murmured with feeling.

Unexpectedly, Maggie felt tears prickle at the backs of her eyes. If only it could be that simple. She and Antony were good together – they were friends as well as lovers and worked well together in the business. If it wasn't for Alexander taking his place firmly at the tip of their triangle, they might well have become a conventional couple; one man, one woman, maybe even children.

It was foolish to even speculate. He might be across the Atlantic, but Alexander wasn't going to disappear in a puff of smoke. His memory was almost as compelling as the man himself.

Forcing herself to smile, Maggie nodded towards the stage. 'I think you'll find this interesting,' she said, directing Antony's attention away from her and towards the stage.

He turned and watched as the dancers eased into a more lyrical mood. Maggie knew he would appreciate the stage-managed seduction about to take place, and she was glad he had happened to call when this particular entertainment was due. Unusually for someone who was normally so attuned to her feelings, Antony seemed totally oblivious to her sudden melancholy. His attention seemed to be taken up entirely by the floor show.

Maggie took a restorative sip of her Martini and pulled herself together. But for a long time as Antony watched the stage, she watched Antony, unaware that, from the shadows by the door, she was being watched in her turn.

Chapter Three

*L*ena saw the expressions which flitted across Maggie's face and felt the sharp, searing stab of jealousy cut through her. Why did Antony have to come? Maggie's feelings were written plainly across her face which was lit by the gentle, flickering light of the candles on the table. Lena could interpret them from across the room, yet Antony seemed oblivious. The man was a fool.

Looking down, she realised that she had curled her hands into fists so tight that her fingernails had broken the skin on her palms. She pressed her hands together to hide the blood, pushing through the door with her shoulder.

In the ladies' cloakroom, Lena rinsed her hands under a tap and stared at herself in the mirror over the basin. Her eyes looked wild, hunted, and she fought to control the feelings which rioted, out of control, through her nervous system. The strength of her anger frightened her and she struggled to modify it, to claw back her grip on normality.

Smiling meaninglessly at the girl who was manning reception, Lena grabbed her bag and slipped through the maintenance door, down into the cellars of the building. The darkness enveloped her like a lover and she was comforted by the steady hum of the heating system as she sank onto her haunches.

She often came here when things got too much, when she wanted to think without being observed. Her fingers were still shaking as she reached into her bag and fumbled for her cigarettes and matches. She was supposed to be giving up, but she always carried emergency supplies, just in case. The crumpled packet at the bottom of her bag was empty. Cursing, she screwed it up in her fist and dropped it on the floor by her feet.

The matches gave a satisfying rattle inside their box as she shook it. Lena smiled. Even as a very small child, she had always enjoyed playing with matches. Her smile hardened as old, unwanted memories tried to push their way to the forefront of her mind. With the benefit of long experience, she shoved them back again and opened the box.

Taking out a match, she gave the small, pink end a ritualistic tap before scraping it slowly along the rough edge. The familiar sound made her feel calmer and she drew it back again, harder this time, so that the sulphur ignited and flickered into flame.

A thrill, almost sexual, ran through her as she watched the tiny pinhead of fire work its way slowly along the match, blowing it out just before it reached her fingers. Dropping the dead match on the floor, Lena struck another. This time she allowed her feelings through as she watched the flame. She was in love with Maggie, wanted her with a passion which burnt slowly within her, day in, day out.

34

Striking a third match, she thought of the bitter-sweet torture of having to work alongside her, not daring to allow her feelings to show. How did Maggie see her? Lena grimaced. As her girl-Friday, she guessed, her ever willing, hard-working factotum. She struck another match viciously and watched with delight as, this time, it flared for a moment, the flame leaping up, blue to orange in one slender streak.

She jumped as she heard a sound above her, afraid for a moment that someone was about to open the maintenance door and discover her. The momentary lapse in her concentration meant that the match had burned right down to her fingertips and she dropped it with a muffled yelp as it burned her.

Sticking the tip of her forefinger and thumb in her mouth, she sucked the small pain away. It was time to go back upstairs before she was missed. Dropping the now half-empty matchbox back in her bag, Lena reluctantly went back upstairs.

In the main room, the guest Lena had identified had already been lured onto the stage. Sara Lawson was obviously game: her face was wreathed in smiles and there was a gleam of anticipation in her large, heavily made-up eyes.

'Is she familiar with the two men?' Antony murmured to Maggie.

Maggie laughed. 'Marc and Jason. They've been in Ms Lawson's room for the past four days,' she told him.

From the avid expression on the young woman's face, she was not in the least bit abashed by allowing an audience to witness what she had been doing ever since she arrived. Glancing around the room, Maggie

35

saw that the guests were divided, roughly fifty-fifty, into those who were watching, and those who were preoccupied with their own companions.

To her left, a woman's attempt to suppress a low, orgasmic groan was only partially successful, and Maggie shot the young man who was responsible a cautionary frown. He should have seen that groan coming and thought of an effective way to muffle it. His client was a particularly private individual who would be mortified if she realised her brief foray into sexual excess had been audible.

Turning her attention back to the stage, Maggie saw that Sara was standing, acquiescent, as the two men slowly stripped the clothes from her body. Not quite *acquiescent*, Maggie corrected herself, smiling; Sara was definitely posing so that as each part of her body was revealed – it was shown to its best advantage.

She had a good body and was clearly aware of it. Though short, she was perfectly in proportion, her legs slightly longer than her torso, her hips balancing the fullness of her breasts below the indentation of her waist. Under the spotlights her white skin looked as though it could have been carved from alabaster, though as it met the heat of the lights it pearled with moisture. Maggie caught herself licking her lips, imagining the salt taste of the woman's skin.

Sara's soft blonde hair fell across her face as Marc kissed her. To Maggie's approval, Jason smoothed it back so that those who were watching had a clear view of the thrust and parry of their tongues. Naked now, Sara pressed herself against the hard, ebony-skinned body of Marc as he kissed her more deeply, bending her over his arm so that her back arched like

36

a bow and she was obliged to cling to him to stop herself from falling.

Maggie chanced a glance at Eleanor Barrington. She was wearing a safe, chic black dress with a small *diamanté* bow brooch pinned discreetly above one breast. Her long legs, clad in black nylon, were pressed neatly together and crossed at the ankles, but she was sitting on the edge of her seat and seemed unable to take her eyes off the woman on the stage.

Marc was caressing Sara's breasts now, lifting them and licking at the large, wine-red areolae with his long tongue. Maggie felt a prickle of arousal as she watched, knowing from experience how Marc's tongue could rasp tantalisingly across the skin. Sara leaned back into Jason's waiting arms, arching her neck so that Marc could lick a path across it. She reached up, over her shoulders to hold Jason round his neck and Marc nuzzled the damp cavity of her armpit.

More of the audience had turned their attention to the stage now, fascinated, it seemed by the almost choreographed seduction taking place. It was obvious that Marc and Jason had not been idle during the long hours spent with Sara in her room. Each knew exactly which buttons to press, every short cut to arousing her.

Sara herself clearly did not need much arousing. Her eyes were half closed in ecstasy, her lips parted moistly as she thrust out her hips, inviting Marc to turn his attention to her pelvis. He took his time, holding her by the waist and rolling his tongue over her hipbones before planting dozens of butterfly-light kisses across her quivering abdomen.

The background music, a tuneless, eerie refrain,

grew softer so that the audience could hear Sara's groans.

'Oh, oh please . . .' she murmured as Marc's long fingers stroked their way down to her lightly furred vulva. 'Kiss me there. Please kiss me there.'

'In front of all these people?' Marc sounded amused, yet indulgent, dipping his tongue into Sara's navel as she gyrated her hips desperately.

'Yes – please, please!'

An expectant hush descended across the room as Marc slowly, gently parted the outer labia to reveal the tender pink flesh hidden within. The communal tension quivered on the air as he bent his head and licked delicately at the dew-soaked folds with the very tip of his tongue.

Maggie felt herself grow warm and she wriggled slightly on her seat. Without looking at her, Antony eased his hand up her skirt and found the warm, moist centre of her. Under the cover of the table, he breached the flimsy defence of her lace panties and sank his middle finger into the hot, wet folds of flesh.

Sara's moans rose steadily to a crescendo as Marc's strokes became firmer and hit their target. Maggie allowed her thighs to fall apart, feeling Antony enter her with his finger and probe the tight channel into her body. Her clitoris throbbed and pressed forward, wanting to feel his touch there, yet not wanting him to withdraw from her body.

Judging by the sighs and glazed expressions around her, Maggie knew she was not the only woman to be experiencing such expert attention. When, at last, Antony began to stimulate the hard bud of her clitoris, she spasmed almost at once. Caging her cries behind her teeth, she bore down on his questing fingers as her orgasm broke and she leaned forward, concentrating on the response of her body.

Minutes later, Sara came, noisily, on the stage. Jason held her fast as she writhed and she sagged against him, momentarily forgetting to pose and present her body to its best advantage.

Recovering herself quickly, Maggie turned her attention to Eleanor. The woman had a fixed expression on her face, as if she was battling to hide her feelings. Her eyes fluttered in alarm as Marc left the stage and walked towards her. For a moment as he held out his hand to her, Maggie thought that she would refuse. Then slowly, as if in a daze, Eleanor put her hand in his and rose shakily to her feet.

A light ripple of applause travelled around the room as the spotlight fell on Eleanor. She blinked owlishly as she stepped onto the stage and was temporarily blinded by the harsh lights. Sara came forward to take her hand, and led her over to the couch which had been brought to centre stage.

Eleanor seemed to be in a trance. Though there was a reluctance about her, she did not hang back as Sara pressed her to sit on the edge of the couch. The audience was treated to a view of Sara's generously proportioned bottom as she crouched down to remove Eleanor's shoes.

Maggie watched intently, ready to rescue Eleanor should she show any sign that she did not want to continue. Despite Lena's assurances, which Maggie knew from past experience she could generally trust, she herself still harboured doubts about this particular guest. It seemed, though, that those doubts could well be unfounded for Eleanor was sitting quite passively on the white linen-covered couch. She still looked as if she didn't quite know what she was doing there, but the tension in the way she held herself was unmistakably due to excitement rather than embarrassment.

Biting her lip nervously, she leaned back against Jason, who had quietly taken up his position behind her on the couch. Sara made way for Marc who knelt at Eleanor's feet, looking up at her as if waiting for some secret signal. He must have received it, for after a moment he ran his fingertips lightly up her thighs and gently pushed the hemline of her dress above her stocking tops.

Everyone in the room focused on the sight of his sensitive, dark-skinned fingers releasing the stockings from the suspenders which restrained them. Eleanor seemed to be holding her breath – in common with much of the audience – as Marc rolled one stocking slowly down her leg. Passing the diaphanous tube of fabric to Sara, he cradled the arch of Eleanor's foot in his palm and bent his head to press his lips to it.

Maggie's eyes moved restlessly across the stage. Sara was watching Marc avidly, pulling the stocking between her two hands and winding the ends around her fingers, stretching it taut. Maggie smiled to herself, recognising the tension building within the other girl as she watched Marc with another woman.

So far Jason had barely moved, merely acting as a support for Eleanor who was sitting motionless on the couch. Now he stroked the long sweep of her neck, caressing the tender dip at her collarbones and brushing his lips against her hair.

Marc began to kiss each of her toes in turn, licking between them and drawing the tip into his mouth. Eleanor let out a low groan, as if taken by surprise by the sensations this produced. She closed her eyes, her expression halfway between anguish and ecstasy, as Marc removed her other stocking and subjected that foot to the same treatment.

Eleanor's dress was pushed up to her waist now, revealing the black, sensible briefs she wore underneath. Maggie was close enough to see that the gusset had been pulled into the crease of her labia, exposing the dark, luxuriant pubic hair which curled around the edges of the elastic. Imagining how the silky fabric would be chafing against the other woman's sensitive vulval flesh, Maggie felt her own interest spark anew.

Antony's thigh pressed close to hers underneath the table and Maggie leaned in towards him, relishing the heat of his body and the feel of hard muscle beneath the crisply tailored fabric of his dinner jacket. Desire spread slowly through her, fed by the visual stimulus of the stage show and the familiarity of the man sitting beside her. It wasn't often she was turned on by the known, the secure, but she relished it all the same, not caring to examine her feelings too closely.

Marc's fingers climbing Eleanor's inner thighs provoked a soft moan from the woman who was now leaning back into Jason's arms. Sara was growing impatient as she watched from the sidelines. Still naked, she seemed oblivious to the watching eyes as she stroked herself with Eleanor's stockings. Back and forth, back and forth she drew the filmy material across her breasts, stimulating the nipples into two hard brown cones which shone under the stage lights.

Eleanor shook her head from side to side as Jason lifted her hips to allow Marc to draw down her panties, but she did not resist, merely shivering as her dress was pushed higher, rolled beneath her arms to expose the creamy expanse of her skin from ankle to black lace bra. She was slender, her thighs were long and smooth-skinned, her belly almost concave between her hipbones which jutted either side.

Sara gave a little mewl of delight as her eyes feasted on the thick black hair which nestled at the apex of her thighs. Marc stroked it with the backs of his fingers, gently as if afraid to startle her. At the same time, Jason stroked her hair away from her face and brushed his lips lightly across her temples.

The background music had thus far been light and unobtrusive, now it shifted subtly so that the beat began to throb. Every woman in the audience was affected by it, as if, as one, their blood had surged in their veins.

The change in Eleanor was dramatic. Throwing back her head, she sought and found Jason's mouth. Wrapping one arm around his head, she kissed him hungrily. Someone in the audience murmured encouragement and Sara draped herself over Marc's broad back, as if the sight of Eleanor's unleashed passion had made her crave the contact of his naked flesh with hers.

Maggie brushed her fingers lightly across the front of Antony's trousers and was unsurprised to feel the tumescence stretching the fabric. She licked her lips, feeling hot as she thought of releasing it later. The sight of the quartet on the stage was arousing her, quietening, for now, the restlessness which had plagued her over the past few months.

Eleanor seemed to have no idea of the true agenda for the evening. Her capitulation to the two men had been relatively easy and Maggie sensed that she was expecting the seduction to progress from there. Her

42

eyes flew open in alarm when she felt Sara's smaller hands replace Marc's on her thighs.

'No,' she cried, starting to sit up.

Jason gentled her, whispering against her hair and stroking her neck. Slipping his hands under the rolled up tube of her dress, he tugged at the lacy cups of her bra so that her breasts spilled out. They were small with neat, dark-pink areolae surrounding button hard nipples. Jason rolled her nipples between his fingers and thumbs, extracting a low moan of submission which echoed round the room.

Not until she heard this signal did Sara begin to make love to Eleanor in earnest.

Marc sat on the far end of the couch where he could watch without obstructing the view of the audience. Jason, having propped Eleanor's near-naked body up with pillows, eased himself away so that Eleanor could concentrate solely on what Sara was doing to her.

Everyone in the room seemed to strain forward as Sara cupped the mound between Eleanor's legs. Slowly, as if relishing every second, she ran her thumbs down the channels on either side of her inner labia before gently peeling them back. The tender, dark-pink skin glistened under the lights, betraying Eleanor's reluctant arousal. Knowing this, she gasped, a small cry of shame escaping from between her lips. A thrill seemed to run through the room.

Eleanor's head fell back on the pillows and her lips parted as Sara began to caress the sensitive folds of skin. Seeking out every secret point of pleasure, she quickly brought the other woman to the very point of orgasm. Judging when the moment had come, she pressed her fingertip lightly against her clitoris and moved the hard bud of flesh against her pubic bone.

Eleanor cried out, drawing her knees up to open herself wider as the first rush of pleasure swamped her. Someone in the audience sighed loudly, as if she empathised with Eleanor's every emotion. Sara waited until the first climax had died before putting her lips to Eleanor's vulva.

'Oh no! No – please – no more . . . aah!'

Though she could not see clearly from where she was sitting, Maggie guessed that the other woman had entered Eleanor's body with her tongue. As she watched, Sara reached up, splayed her hands over Eleanor's exposed breasts and began to play with them, rubbing and tweaking the softening nipples back to hardness.

A fine film of sweat had broken out on Eleanor's skin and she opened her legs wider, her actions belying the soft cries of denial that were still whispering from her lips.

'Please don't – oh God in Heaven! I can't – yes – oh yes! Deeper . . .!'

Her fingers meshed in Sara's hair as a second orgasm, far deeper than the first, washed over her. Scissoring her hips over the other woman's narrow shoulders, she mashed her pelvis against her face, grinding her clitoris against her nose and urging her tongue in deeper. By the time Sara resurfaced, she was panting, but triumphant. She kissed Eleanor full on the lips, holding her at the back of her head so that Eleanor couldn't turn away.

From the corner of her eye, Maggie saw Derry rise from his table and kiss each of his women in turn. One of them pouted prettily as he whispered to her, a second scowled, her eyes hard on the third woman as Derry took her by the hand and led her away.

'One at a time, eh?' Antony murmured, noticing the exchange at the same time as Maggie.

Maggie turned to him and smiled. 'You can stop speculating, Tony darling – he'll have plenty of stamina for all three. He won't need any help, which is just as well because tonight I'm reserving you for myself.'

Antony watched her lips as she spoke, his eyes shadowed by desire. Maggie felt a fresh rush of arousal as he leaned forward and kissed her, too gently, on the mouth. He chuckled softly as she tried to press her lips harder against his, drawing away slightly and catching her by the chin with his thumb and forefinger.

'Greedy!' he admonished softly, rubbing the pad of his thumb across the sensitive swell of her lower lip.

'I'll make you pay for that later,' she retorted huskily, turning her eyes back to the stage.

Marc and Jason had unobtrusively melted into the shadows, leaving Sara to coax Eleanor on to her back on the white couch. She was completely naked now, as was Sara still, and the two of them provided a visual feast to the spellbound audience. The sight of Sara lying prone on top of Eleanor, breast to breast, hip to hip, mouth to mouth, was bewitching. The atmosphere in the room was highly charged, as if all the watchers were transfixed by the tableau before them, forgetting everything but sensation as they shared in the experiences of the two women on the stage. In the corners of the room, the shadows shifted as couples danced sensuously, oblivious to all but the erotic slip of one body against another.

Sweat glistened on Sara's back as she slid her body slowly up Eleanor's until she was virtually straddling her face. Eleanor lay passively and stared up, almost certainly for the first time, at another woman's sex. Slowly, her tongue slid between her lips and ran along them, moistening the skin. Sara smiled and, reaching between her legs, she opened herself to her lover's gaze.

Supporting herself on her knees on either side of Eleanor's head, Sara slowly lowered herself until her vulva touched Eleanor's lips. Tentatively at first, the other woman probed the slippery flesh with the very tip of her tongue. Gradually, as she accustomed herself to the taste, she began to rotate her tongue round, lapping at the delicate folds with increasing enthusiasm.

Sara gathered up her own breasts in her hands and began to knead and caress them. From Sara's expression Maggie could tell that Eleanor was learning fast. As she watched, Eleanor reached up to cradle Sara's buttocks in her hands so that she could gain more control. While she tongued her, she began to squeeze the spongy flesh of her bottom, widening the crease so that the small opening of her anus was exposed.

As if on cue, Jason reappeared on the stage with a small tube of lubricant. Sara shuddered as he worked a generous amount into her crease. Eleanor stopped what she was doing for a moment and Maggie saw her eyes widen in disbelief as she saw what Jason was doing. For a split second, Maggie thought that Eleanor would decide enough was enough and pull away, but the sight of Jason's erect, condom-encased penis probing at Sara's anus seemed to tip her over the edge from mere arousal to uncontrollable lust.

Her own legs opened reflexively, her pelvis push-

46

ing upward so that her open sex could rub against Jason's hair-roughened thigh as he knelt between them.

Sara cried out as he eased into her, her cry turning into a sob of pure pleasure as Eleanor thrust her tongue into the silky passage of her vagina. As Jason moved carefully in and out of Sara's back passage, Eleanor's tongue moved busily from her vagina to Jason's scrotum and back again, flicking up to her clitoris for good measure.

Maggie suddenly felt an urgent need to get away from the almost claustrophobic atmosphere in the room and indulge her own needs somewhere more private.

'Have you seen enough?' she whispered to Antony.

He looked at her quizzically and, recognising the feverish glitter in her eyes, nodded quickly.

'Let's go outside, then.'

The trio on the stage came in quick succession, one after the other as Maggie and Antony rose and turned away. Their gasps and cries followed them out of the room, giving impetus to their steps, driving them out through the rear foyer and into the soft, velvet darkness of the summer night.

'It was hot in there,' Maggie said as she looked up at the stars.

Antony's hand slipped between the soft fall of her hair and the nape of her neck. He caressed the tender skin thoughtfully, sending little ripples of pleasure through her body.

'What is it, Maggie? What's wrong?'

Maggie turned to him, frowning in confusion. 'I don't know, I just . . .' she shrugged and gave a small, uncertain laugh. 'Let's walk a little way.'

Antony said nothing more, though she felt his eyes

resting thoughtfully on her several times as they strolled around the building to the long terrace at the side. It was quieter there, away from the main ball-room where Maggie knew there would now be dancing for those who still had energy to spare after the floor show.

The double French doors leading from the library to the terrace were standing open and Antony went to close them. Maggie sat on the vast, floral chintz-covered swing-seat out on the terrace and looked out across the grounds to the gravel driveway which curved round out of sight to the front of the hotel.

'Penny for them?' Antony sat down beside her, making the seat rock.

Maggie leaned against him, nestling into the warm circle of his arms as they came about her. 'I was just thinking that for all that there are dozens of people inside, when you're out here you could be completely alone.'

'And you like that idea?'

'Mmm. Sometimes.' She sighed, enjoying the sensation of Antony's fingertips circling lightly on her bare arm.

'The exhibitionist in you needs a rest every now and then, I guess?'

Maggie laughed softly. 'You could be right. Sometimes . . .'

'What?'

'Oh nothing. Take no notice of me. Antony?'

'Hmm?'

'Would you do something for me?'

Antony turned and looked down at her, tipping up her chin slightly so that he could see her face.

'What's that?'

'Make love to me?'

48

His lips curved into a smile. 'Did you think I wouldn't?'

'You don't understand. I want you to make love to me as if it was the very first time.'

Dipping his head, Antony kissed her lightly on the lips. 'Do you remember the very first time you and I made love?'

Maggie smiled, remembering that it was Antony with whom she had watched her first 'exhibition', and how uninhibited her reaction to his advances had been.

'Of course. But I don't mean I want a repeat of the real first time. I just want to feel as if it's new again. Can you understand?'

Stroking her face, Antony regarded her thoughtfully. 'I think so. You want to make love for yourself, not because it's expected of you.'

'Partly, yes.' Maggie closed her eyes as Antony kissed her again, allowing the warm, liquid langour to flow through her limbs. 'Don't you ever want tenderness – want it to mean something?'

Antony's face darkened slightly and Maggie realised she had made him think of Alexander. She was surprised by the small stab of pain the realisation caused her. He said nothing to confirm her suspicions though. Instead he smiled slightly.

'It always means something when it's with you, Maggie.'

There was a thread of sincerity in his voice that made Maggie's heart tighten in her chest, and at that moment she realised that Antony probably shared her half-formed yearning for a 'normal' love affair. Gazing into his eyes in the darkness, Maggie understood that it was something of which they would never speak, that it would remain an unspoken bond between them. Reaching up, she curled her fingers in the hair at the nape of his neck and eased his head down to hers.

The kiss started gently, lovingly, but quickly turned into something more. As the passion surged through her veins, making every centimetre of her skin prickle with awareness, Maggie turned so that she was half lying across his lap. Her hair fell forward across his face, her breasts flattened against the hard wall of his chest and his arms came about her, pressing her close.

Maggie groaned and insinuated her tongue between his lips. His mouth tasted of red wine with an underlying sweetness which made her hungry for more. The small sound he made at the back of his throat as she kissed him thrilled her and she ground her mouth harder against his, pushing his lips against his teeth.

Her aggression was exciting him, pumping adrenalin through his veins and that excitement transmitted itself to Maggie, making her feel hot and restless. The seat swung crazily as she knelt astride his lap and she clung to him, laughing down into his passion-flushed face.

His desire for her was so plain, so uncomplicated it made her happy just to look at him. Slowly, holding his eye, Maggie pushed her dress off her shoulders. Antony's eyes flickered away from hers to rove the curve of her shoulder. It was milky white in the darkness, her skin spangled by starlight as she eased the dress down to her waist.

Her bare breasts hardened in response to the kiss of the night air and Maggie immediately brought her own hands up to cup and caress them. Her nipples sprang to life against her fingertips as she caressed them and she felt Antony's cock leap in his pants in response.

Smiling to herself, Maggie bent from the waist and offered one nipple to him.

'Suck,' she whispered.

Antony obliged, drawing the tumescent nub between his lips and sucking gently on it, swirling his tongue around the puckered skin. Maggie sighed, fingering her other nipple lazily as Antony's warm, wet mouth drew a response from deep in her womb.

His hands were restless against her waist, pushing at the roll of fabric sitting at the top of her hips. After a few moments, Maggie straightened and her breast was pulled from his mouth. It was shiny with saliva, the nipple coaxed to a hungering peak by his lips and tongue.

Climbing off the swing-seat, Maggie undulated her hips so that she could push the dress down her legs to her ankles. Stepping out of it, she kicked it carelessly aside and smiled seductively at him.

Antony's eyes narrowed as he gazed at her, naked now save for the ridiculously high-heeled sandals.

'Jesus, Maggie,' he breathed, 'you're magnificent!'

'You've seen me like this often enough,' she teased, aware that her voice, like his, was hoarse with longing.

Antony shook his head, his eyes lingering on the vulnerable depilated flesh at the apex of her thighs. 'I forget. Or I tell myself that my memory exaggerates. Come here and let me feel you.'

Maggie took a step forward, gasping as Antony cupped her sex with his hand, his fingers slipping easily into the soft channels of her flesh.

'So wet,' he whispered. 'So hot.'

'Taste me.'

He smiled. 'All in good time.'

Maggie stood, motionless in the moonlight as Antony ran his fingertips lovingly all over her body, as if re-acquainting himself with every line and contour. Her skin tingled where he had touched so that before too long Maggie felt her entire body was buzzing, over-sensitised, ready for more than this gentle touch. She stiffened slightly as she thought she heard a sound beyond the bushes.

'What is it?' Antony asked at once, not pausing in his leisurely exploration of her sex.

'Nothing,' she said, aware that her control was swiftly slipping away. 'I just thought I heard someone . . .'

Antony smiled mockingly. 'Are you shy?'

Realising that if there was anyone there, it was unlikely to be anyone who was not connected to the hotel, Maggie shook her head. She gasped as Antony's fingers circled the stiffening bud of her clitoris. It didn't matter if there *was* someone there; she generally enjoyed making love in front of others.

Closing her eyes as Antony leaned forward and pressed his lips against the sticky-sweet crease of her labia, she resolutely ignored the prickle of awareness that ran down her spine, telling her that they were not alone in the secretive darkness.

Antony's tongue probed between the tightly furled folds of flesh and Maggie shivered compulsively. If he did that too often she would come, too quickly. Taking the initiative, she pushed Antony back, against the cushions. His eyes opened wide, surprise and amusement chasing across them.

'What?'

'Lie still,' Maggie said feverishly.

Antony obeyed her, watching through hooded eyes

as she dispensed with the fastenings to his trousers and pulled them down. His shirt partially covered his erection and she pushed it aside with a growl of impatience. Recognising her mood, Antony felt a fresh rush of desire and his cock twitched and began to throb.

He sighed raggedly as Maggie ran her palm too briefly along its length. Pulling at his buttons, she opened his shirt, her long fingernails scratching at his skin. Sensing her impatience, Antony lay still as she straddled him. It had been a while since he had allowed himself to be used like this, but he found that he wanted it. God how he wanted it!

Positioning the circumcised bulb of his penis at the entrance to her body, Maggie let it rest there for a few seconds, chafing lightly against the stretched membranes. He felt her warm juices bathing him, running down the shaft of his cock, anointing him ready for communion. Maggie's expression was intent, her body taut as a bow as she arched her back and sank down on him.

She groaned as he pierced her, moving her buttocks from side to side to pull him in deeper. Antony felt the sweat break out on his skin. It was too intense, almost painfully so, and his breathing became harsher, his mouth and throat running dry.

'Maggie . . .'

She made a sound, halfway between a command and a question and Antony leaned back on the pillows, closing his eyes.

Maggie's attention had turned inwards and she had to concentrate to remind herself that this was Antony, that she had wanted to share tenderness with him. But the momentum was gathering pace and emotion was squeezed out by the strength of her desire. At that moment all that mattered to her was the potency of that throbbing shaft which skewered her every time she moved her hips up and down.

God but it was good! Antony's cock filled her, stretching the elastic walls of her vagina and stimulating each and every tiny nerve ending. She felt as though she was consumed by heat, taken over by a conflagration that urged her on, harder, faster, cruder.

'Oh sweet Jesus. Maggie, Maggie – ah.'

Antony jerked upright, putting his arms around her and burying his face in the damp valley between her breasts as he came. Maggie squirmed feverishly in his lap, bearing down until the desperate rush to climax peaked and the electric thrills raced through her from head to toe.

They remained like that, pressed together for several moments. It was Antony who broke the silence.

'Do you think whoever was watching got value for money?' he said wryly.

Maggie had forgotten that she had felt they were being observed. Now she pulled away from Antony slightly and frowned, listening. 'I probably imagined it,' she said.

Antony caught her face between his hands and kissed her lingeringly. 'I love you,' he murmured.

'Mmm. Me too.' Maggie smiled, aware of some of her former wistfulness returning. 'Antony – ' She stopped short as she heard something close by. A discordant clang, swiftly silenced.

Quickly, they separated and pulled on their clothes, just as a motorbike pulled away from the main part of the building and roared off along the drive, sending a spray of gravel flying through the air.

Maggie's mouth ran dry as she stared after him,

sure that she had seen that motorbike before. And she knew, with an unshakeable conviction, that it had been the biker from the estuary who had watched her making love with Antony.

She turned, anger making her eyes blaze and her mouth tighten.

'Are you sure it was him?' Antony said, reading her mind.

'What do you think?' she hissed. 'Well I hope he enjoyed himself – nasty little pervert.'

'Maggie,' Antony laughed, 'you didn't mind someone watching until you realised it was him.'

Maggie flushed, embarrassed by her own hypocrisy. 'It's different,' she muttered stubbornly.

'Why?'

'It just is.'

How could she explain to Antony that the idea of the biker seeing her like that made her feel exposed, vulnerable in a way she never experienced even during her more flamboyant public antics? Perhaps it was something to do with the fact that the biker had shown her contempt, that to see her like that would have undoubtedly amused him, but belittled her.

'I don't bloody care what he thinks of me,' she said aloud.

'I should think not,' Antony retorted, clearly amused at her agitation.

Maggie turned on him, ready to give him a piece of her mind, but the appearance of Gina, the receptionist, at the door to the library pulled her up short. There was something about the girl's face, anxious and flushed, that made Maggie hurry to meet her at the French doors.

'Gina – what's wrong?'

'There's a fire – '

'A fire?' Maggie interrupted, her voice rising.

'I've called the fire brigade and Lena's gone down with the extinguisher.' The girl sounded breathless, her anxiety about the fire compounded by her eagerness to have been seen to do the right thing.

'Lena? Where is this fire?'

'In the maintenance room.'

Maggie glanced at Antony and together they pushed past Gina and went inside.

Chapter Four

'Why hasn't the alarm sounded?' Maggie demanded as the three of them rushed towards the door to the maintenance area.

'Lena turned it off. She said there was no need to cause a panic, that she'd sort it out. She told me not to call the fire brigade, but I thought . . . I did do the right thing, didn't I, Maggie?'

Seeing that the girl was virtually ringing her hands, Maggie took the time to stop and reassure her.

'You did absolutely the right thing. Now please sound the alarm. We must evacuate the building before the fire brigade arrives or they'll wonder what the hell we're playing at.'

Gina ran back to the reception desk and switched on the fire alarm. Immediately, the discordant clang echoed throughout the hotel and Maggie knew that her staff would begin to lead the guests to safety, just as they had practised during numerous drills.

Antony had already reached the entrance to the maintenance area.

'Don't open the door, Tony,' Maggie said in alarm. 'The fire brigade are on their way, let them deal with it.'

'I thought you said Lena was down there?' he said, glancing at Gina for confirmation.

'Yes – she took the fire extinguisher from underneath the reception desk.'

Antony opened his mouth to say that he would go in after her, but just then the siren of the fire engine sounded, louder and louder as it drew to a halt in front of the hotel.

Maggie stepped forward as some half-dozen burly men in uniform burst through the door, filling the foyer with an air of purposeful activity.

'Where's the fire?' The speaker was broad and thickly set, his white helmet and stripes denoting his rank.

'In here.' Antony indicated the door to the maintenance area. 'There's a woman down there with a fire extinguisher.'

The officer in charge muttered something vicious under his breath and signalled to two of his men.

'If you'd evacuate the building yourselves now please sir – madam,' he ordered nodding at Maggie.

For a moment Maggie thought that Antony was going to stand his ground, but thankfully common sense won over whatever other emotions he was experiencing. He followed Maggie and Gina outside, leaving the experts to their work.

Sensing that he needed to feel he was doing something useful, Maggie asked him to run the head count on the guests and staff while she waited anxiously for news of Lena. What had the girl been thinking of, going down to tackle the blaze herself like that? Since the hotel first opened, Maggie had made a point of underlining the importance of safety to her staff, including fire drills so frequent that she knew all would act automatically whenever the alarm sounded.

'Are you sure Lena told you not to sound the alarm?' she asked Gina, puzzled by the way her normally responsible second-in-command had flouted the most basic of rules.

'Oh yes. I thought it was odd, but she insisted that it wasn't worth it. It was only a small fire, she said, and she could deal with it easily herself without needing to call out the fire brigade. Honestly, Maggie, Lena made it seem as if I was making a fuss over nothing . . .' the girl trailed off miserably, and Maggie realised she thought she was being blamed for the breach of procedure.

'It's all right, Gina – you did the right thing by coming to find me, I only – '

Maggie stopped abruptly as she realised that the other girl was looking past her, a look of horror on her face. Whirling round, Maggie saw that Lena was being carried between two firemen. She appeared to be unconscious and her clothes and hair were blackened. They lay her gently on the grass just as an ambulance arrived. Maggie reached her side at the same time as the paramedics.

'Oh my God!' she gasped, fearing the worst.

'She'll be all right, miss,' the paramedic said, his eyes never leaving Lena as he strapped an oxygen mask to her face. 'Looks like she's inhaled a fair bit of smoke. We'll take her to A and E to be on the safe side. They'll probably keep her in overnight for observation.'

Lena spluttered and opened her eyes. Her gaze

locked onto Maggie's, a curious kind of pleading in their depths that tugged at Maggie's heart.

'You'll be all right,' she soothed, dropping to her knees beside her as they waited for the stretcher to take her away. 'I'll come down to the hospital just as soon as I've seen to things here.'

Lena clutched at her hand, her grip surprisingly strong, her eyes pleading as she was lifted onto the stretcher. Maggie had to gently prise her hand away as the paramedics carried Lena to the waiting ambulance. Maggie stared after her, touched by the anguish she had seen in the other woman's eyes.

'Was that Lena?' Antony joined her as the ambulance pulled away.

'Yes. Nothing serious, apparently, but they'll keep her in 'til morning. Have you finished the head count?'

'I have. All present and correct as far as I can tell. And I understand the fire has been put out – we'd better go inside.' He touched her arm when she didn't respond. 'Are you all right, Maggie? You look pale.'

Maggie pulled her thoughts away from Lena with an effort and turned her attention to the more immediate concern of speaking to the fire officer. As they reached the door, one of the guests marched up and barred their way.

'What's going on?' she demanded imperiously.

'Everything is under control Mrs Jannsen,' Maggie said soothingly, though everything in her prickled with irritation. Couldn't the woman see that she was busy?

Antony came to her rescue. 'Let me find you a bench, Mrs Jannsen,' he said, taking her by the arm and manoeuvring her away from the hotel. 'We can have a sit down and a chat – just the two of us.'

Lysa Jannsen looked Antony up and down assessingly, then her expression softened and the arrogance slipped away. It made her look ten years younger.

'Very well,' she said, shooting a self-satisfied glance at Maggie. I had hoped to speak with Maggie, but I'm sure you'll do just as well.'

'I shall do my best,' Antony assured her. As they walked away, he threw a look at Maggie over his shoulder and rolled his eyes.

'Thank you,' she mouthed, blowing him a small kiss before continuing on her way to meet the fire officer.

He was waiting for her in the foyer. 'We'll be off now, miss. I'm afraid there's a bit of a mess down there, but no permanent damage as far as I can tell. You were lucky.'

'Yes, thank you, Officer . . .?'

'Tunnock. Brett Tunnock.' He smiled and Maggie could not help but notice that his eyes, glittering at her from the crinkles of his laughter lines, were a deep, soulful blue. She returned the smile, holding out her hand.

Brett Tunnock removed the glove of his right hand and enclosed hers in a firm handshake. Maggie liked the feel of his skin against hers. It was warm and dry with just the right hint of roughness that she would have expected of a man with such a physical job. She liked a man with a firm handshake and she found herself speculating as to whether the rest of his body, hidden beneath the thick, black serge uniform would be equally as firm.

'I'll need to make an inspection visit sometime later this week,' he said, making Maggie aware that she was holding on to his hand for just a fraction of a second too long. She smiled ruefully and let him have it back.

'I'll look forward to it,' she murmured, secretly pleased by the way the older man's eyes narrowed in recognition. He seemed to have to make an effort to recover himself, but when he did, his tone was brisk.

'We'll have to investigate further, but from what I've seen so far, I'd say that the fire was deliberate.'

Maggie's eyes widened and all her lecherous thoughts about the man in front of her fled. 'Deliberate?' she repeated incredulously. 'You mean that someone might have purposefully lit a fire in the hotel?'

Brett shrugged. Taking off his white helmet, he passed his forearm across his forehead wearily before putting it back on again.

'There were several spent matches on the floor, as if someone had been striking and discarding them. Maybe there was litter or some other flammable object on the ground, something that would catch light. We'll see. I'll contact you shortly Miss . . .?'

'Maggie. Call me Maggie.' She smiled faintly at him, watching him thoughtfully as she walked away.

Antony came to join her. 'You're looking very pensive,' he said, brushing her hair away from the nape of her neck.

'He thinks that someone might have started the fire on purpose.'

'What?'

'That was my reaction. Who would want to do something like that?' She rubbed wearily at her temples which were beginning to throb. Outside, she could see the guests being shepherded back into the hotel, some complaining loudly at the interruption to their evening, others, their eyes bright with excitement, clearly excited by the unexpected diversion. Danger from a safe distance. Maggie was exhausted.

'Come on – it's past midnight. You look as though you need some rest,' Antony told her.

'I promised Lena I'd go to the hospital.'

'Not now. Be reasonable, Maggie – no one will let you in at this hour. I'll drive you in the morning.'

She sighed heavily. 'There's no need, I'll take my car – I'll need it if I'm to bring Lena home. Thanks anyway. Tony?'

'Hmm?'

'Just before the fire started, do you remember hearing the motorbike?'

They began to walk up the stairs to Maggie's suite.

'Yeah. You thought it might have been your mad biker.'

'Yes. You don't think . . .?'

Antony paused, turning to her with incredulous eyes.

'That he started the fire?'

Maggie nodded.

'That's a pretty wild accusation, Maggie. Whatever makes you think it could have been him on the bike, never mind pegging him as an arsonist, if that is what we've got on our hands?'

'I know, I'm probably letting my imagination run away with me,' she conceded. 'You're right, I *am* tired.'

'We'll talk about it tomorrow when we've had a chance to get some sleep.'

She nodded. 'All right. Good night Antony.'

Maggie went to her room, hurriedly brushed her teeth and fell into bed. The events of the evening had left her completely drained, yet still her mind spun with questions. It wasn't a pleasant feeling to know that someone might have deliberately set fire to the hotel, injuring one of her staff in the process. And whatever Antony said, Maggie knew it had been the biker she had seen roaring away just after the fire had been discovered. There would be a great many questions to be answered in the morning.

'It's quite a mess, isn't it?'

Maggie looked up as Antony joined her in the maintenance room and raised her hands palm upwards in a gesture of helplessness.

'I can't believe the amount of damage that can be caused by one small fire!'

The air was still heavy with the acrid smell of smoke. The metal pipes and the floor around her were blackened and twisted and the caretaker had just left after giving Maggie a sombre report on the cost of repairs.

'Come upstairs,' Antony said gently.

Maggie nodded and followed him up to the foyer.

'Are you ready to leave?' she asked him, looking round for his case.

'Yes, I've packed everything in the car.' Taking both her hands in his, Antony scanned her face, concern sharpening his gaze. 'I could stay for a couple more days if you need me to?'

Maggie had the sudden, overwhelming urge to lay her head on his chest and agree. It struck her that it would be rather wonderful, for once, to surrender the responsibility for the hotel, just for a little while. Instead she shook her head and smiled.

'That's kind of you, Tony, but you must get back to the club. Everything is under control here.'

'Even you?'

Maggie's eyes widened. 'What's that supposed to mean?'

Antony chuckled softly and kissed her. 'Nothing. You'll call me if you need anything?'

'Of course. Go on – if you hang around much longer you'll run into the lunchtime traffic.'

Antony grimaced. 'Okay, hint taken. You will take care, though, Maggie, won't you? Don't overdo things.'

'Stop fussing. I must get into the hospital to see Lena – when I 'phoned earlier they said she could be discharged today.'

'That's good news.' Antony smiled and walked with her to the door. 'Don't be too hard on her – she's obviously paid for her idiocy in going to put out the fire herself.'

'Mm. Actually, I thought she was rather brave.'

'But reckless. Just think what could have happened had the fire brigade not arrived when they did.'

Maggie shuddered. 'It doesn't bear thinking about!'

'Quite. Ciao, Maggie. I'll be in touch.'

'Bye.'

Maggie watched as he strode away, determinedly suppressing the pang of regret that hit her as he left. There was no time for sentimentality – if she was going to pick up Lena it had better be before lunch-time got underway.

Lena saw Maggie arrive and go to talk to the ward sister. Her heart began to beat wildly in her chest, a mixture of pleasure at seeing her, and apprehension about what she would say. Would she be terribly angry with her? Maggie's anger, directed at her, was a hideous prospect.

The night before, when Gina had told her she could

smell smoke, Lena thought she would pass out with terror. She hadn't *meant* to start a fire, not this time. Opening the door to the maintenance room even a crack had told her that something had gone seriously wrong. She'd panicked, grabbing the extinguisher and running to try to control what was happening. She hadn't expected it to get out of hand as quickly as it did. Nor was she prepared for the heat which seared her lungs, nor the smoke that obscured her vision and made breathing impossible.

'Lena?'

She looked up as Maggie called her name. Maggie smiled. 'How are you feeling?'

'Fine,' she croaked, coughing to hide her embarrassment at the hoarseness of her voice.

Maggie was wearing a loose, silk shirt in pale orange over white lycra leggings which emphasised the shapeliness of her legs. Her make-up was light, understated, her dark hair drawn simply off her face and fastened at the nape by an apricot-coloured chiffon scarf. Lena thought she had never looked more beautiful, and it was all she could do not to stare.

'Well, you certainly gave me a fright,' Maggie said brightly, drawing up a chair. 'For a moment there I thought I'd lost you.'

Lena's heart gave a little flip. Could it be that Maggie reciprocated her feelings? It plummeted again as she laughed and quipped, 'After all, the hotel would collapse around our ears without my right-hand woman.'

Lena managed a sickly smile, only half listening as Maggie explained that they had only to wait for the consultant to do his rounds, then she would be able to take her home. Was that really all she was to

Maggie – an efficient employee? Lena, strong as her feelings were towards Maggie, couldn't believe that the other woman didn't reciprocate, at least in part. It was no good, she was going to have to risk Maggie's ridicule and say something.

'Maggie,' she said, interrupting her mid-sentence, 'I – I've been meaning to ask you – to tell you – I . . .'

Both women looked round as the consultant appeared at the end of the bed, several acolytes clustering round him, and the moment was gone.

Maggie glanced at Lena as they drove back to the hotel and frowned. Something was obviously bothering her; it wasn't like her to be this quiet.

'Are you sure you feel well enough to go home?' she asked her. 'We could always take you back again, if not.'

'I'm fine – really. Like the nurse said; a day or two taking it easy and I'll be back to work in no time.'

She sounded cheerful enough, but Maggie could not seem to rid herself of the impression that it was forced. She gave a mental shrug.

'Don't worry – I'll look after you – just so long as you promise never to put yourself in danger like that again'

She paused to concentrate on a particularly badly laid out set of road works. Once they were through them, she felt Lena's eyes resting on her and she glanced quizzically at her. The other girl's eyes were shining, her expression rapt, as if Maggie had offered her the most wonderful gift in the world.

'Will you really?' she breathed.

'Will I really what?' Maggie asked, disconcerted.

'Look after me. Yourself.'

'Of course.' Maggie laughed lightly. Lena's slavish

67

expression was making her feel unaccountably nervous. 'What else are friends for?' She threw a brief smile in Lena's direction before turning her attention back to the road. After a few minutes, Lena said softly,

'We *are* friends, aren't we Maggie? I mean, as well as being employer and employee.'

'Of course,' Maggie replied brightly, wondering where this was leading. But Lena said nothing more, merely settling back more comfortably in her seat. When Maggie chanced to glance at her again, she had her eyes closed and she guessed that she was dozing.

At the hotel, George and Marc were waiting to help Lena up the stairs.

'I'll be up in a minute, Lena, when I've collected my messages,' Maggie told her.

She watched as the two men fussed over her, noticing that Lena tolerated rather than enjoyed their attention. Come to think of it, her assistant had never shown much interest in the 'waiters' they employed, nor, for that matter, in the 'waitresses', so it was difficult in a way to know which sex interested her.

Maggie brought herself up short. What on earth was she thinking about? There was Lena having to be helped up to her room because she was still suffering the after-effects of smoke inhalation, and all Maggie could do was speculate on her sexuality. Shaking her head, she turned away and dealt with what little business requiring her attention had built up in her absence.

Going upstairs, Maggie knocked on the door of the staff bedroom assigned to Lena, waiting for her hoarse 'come in' before entering.

The staff bedrooms were of a similar size to those enjoyed by the guests, though the furniture and furnishings were less luxurious. Nevertheless, Lena's was a comfortable room. Glancing round, Maggie saw that all her belongings were neatly stowed in the cream-coloured wardrobe and chest. The matching dressing table which sat under the window was neatly set with Lena's brush and comb and a small box of cosmetics.

It occurred to Maggie as she went to close the curtains that it could have been anyone's bedroom, it was so excessively tidy. There were no posters on the walls, or personal photographs scattered in frames around the room. There was nothing, in fact, that reminded her of Lena at all. Except for the woman herself, who was sitting in the bed, propped up by pillows.

'How are you now?' she asked her, smiling.

Scanning her face, she saw that Lena looked very pale, a fact that emphasised the dark-blue smudges of fatigue under her eyes. Maggie could see the light freckles which spattered her skin more easily than when she was her usual colour. She was wearing a functional blue and white striped nightshirt, crisply ironed, the collar turned up to frame her face.

'I'm fine, really,' she said, though Maggie noticed that her bottom lip quivered slightly on the final word.

Concerned, she walked over and sat down on the bed before laying her hand gently on Lena's forehead. It was cool, not at all feverish, though her eyes, as they met hers, were bright as two green jewels, glittering in the dim light.

'I think you ought to rest,' Maggie suggested gently. 'When I've finished with the dinner period, I'll look in on you and see if there's anything you might need. Meanwhile, telephone for room service if you want anything. All right?'

Lena nodded, laying her head back on the pillows and closing her eyes as Maggie stroked the hair away from her face. It felt springy under her fingers, yet soft. She stopped reluctantly, and stood up.

'I must go.'

She made sure that Lena was comfortable and that drinks and the telephone were near at hand. At the door, she paused and turned. Lena was watching her, though her eyelids were drooping and she was clearly struggling to stay awake. Her face was shadowed in the half light, her skin almost luminous in the gloom. Maggie felt a short, unexpected jab of desire as she looked at her.

'I'll be back later,' she whispered.

Lena's lips lifted slightly at the corners and Maggie slipped out of the room. As she walked along the corridor, back towards the main part of the hotel, Maggie could not forget the look in the other woman's eyes as she had left. They had been shining, bright with an emotion that Maggie had seen displayed in many others' eyes, many other times, but never in Lena's.

Maggie's interest quickened. Lena desired her and, to her surprise, since she had never thought of the girl in that light before, Maggie found the idea excited her.

Chapter Five

*T*he talk at dinner was still largely about the drama of the night before. Somehow word had spread through the guests that the fire might have been started deliberately and already, to Maggie's dismay, two clients had curtailed their stay and checked out.

Her smile as she entered the dining room was forced and by the time she had gone from table to table, reassuring the guests already assembled there, she felt drained. Brett Tunnock had telephoned earlier to tell her he would be making a thorough fire inspection the following day and she was not looking forward to it. Though she was confident that the fire safety standards at the hotel were as high as they had been at the last routine inspection, it was rather like spotting a police speed-check point and feeling guilty even when within the speed limit. Maggie grimaced to herself and signalled to the barman.

'Martini, please, Derry. A large one.'

Derry flashed her his wide, devil-may-care grin and produced the drink with a flourish. 'That'll be good for what ails you, Maggie,' he said, leaning his elbows on the bar and turning the full force of his hypnotic blue gaze on her.

'What makes you think that something ails me?' Maggie said, amused.

'Experience.' He tapped the side of his nose with his forefinger. 'I can usually tell when a beautiful woman has troubles in her soul.'

Maggie laughed. 'You're flirting with me.'

Derry straightened, disconcerted. 'Can you blame me?'

Maggie looked at him, remembering his charm when she had interviewed him – and the delicious shock of finding him to be the most well-endowed man she had ever come across. She smiled, leaning forward to run her finger down the side of his face, drawing him closer to her.

'Save it for the guests,' she whispered, taking the sting out of the implied rebuke by kissing him, lingeringly, on the lips.

His eyes darkened, the pupils dilating as he held her gaze. His lower lip trembled slightly as she drew away.

'Oh, I do, Maggie. I do. But that doesn't mean my mind doesn't stray every now and then to my boss.'

Maggie chuckled. 'The trouble with *your* mind, Derry, is that it lives permanently in your trousers.'

He grinned, unoffended. 'Another Martini?'

'Why not?'

After a while Maggie felt sufficiently mellow to eat. She ordered a small steak with salad followed by tiny strawberry meringue hearts smothered in thick double cream. Normally, being gregarious by nature, she disliked eating alone, but tonight she was glad of the solitude. She felt restless, hyperactive almost, and she couldn't quite pinpoint the cause.

Glancing at her wristwatch, she decided to make one last tour of inspection of the hotel before going up to check on Lena. *Lena.* Thinking of the other girl caused a *frisson* of awareness to travel along her spine. Something had changed between them since she had recognised the look of longing the other girl had given her. Somehow, Maggie guessed, things would never quite be the same again.

She thought of how Lena had gradually made herself indispensable; running the hotel in her absence, generally making sure that Maggie's life was relatively trouble free. Even to the extent of laying out her clothes and massaging her neck. Maggie closed her eyes for an instant, amazed that she had not seen the signs before. Maybe it was just that she had been too preoccupied to see what had been going on beneath her very nose. With a sigh, she rose from the table and went to do her rounds.

The night receptionist jumped as Maggie entered the foyer, visibly straightening her back and summoning a vacant smile.

'Good evening Maggie,' she said, her voice young and breathless.

Maggie frowned slightly, noticing the way the girl's neat uniform blouse was crumpled, her make-up a little too slap-dash. Making a mental note to mention it to Lena, who was in charge of all the front of house staff, Maggie nodded curtly at her. 'Good evening.'

Passing through the lobby towards the outer doors, she grimaced to herself as she remembered that, Lena being out of commission for the time being, disciplining the girl would fall to her in any case, so she might just as well have got it over with.

The hotel security light clicked on the minute she stepped into range, flooding the courtyard outside with light. The night was bright and clear, a full moon illuminating the shadowed corners of the garden. Glancing swiftly around, Maggie satisfied herself that all appeared to be in order. Deciding to make a quick check of the wine cellar, she took the key from her pocket and went over to the outer door at the side of the hotel.

As she touched the door, it swung inward. Maggie sucked in her breath. Glancing at her watch she saw that it was past midnight. The cellar-man would have finished his business inside hours before – who on earth could be inside at this time of night?

She considered going back to the hotel to summon reinforcements, then a sound from below made her pause. It was low and resonant: the unmistakable sound of a woman's pleasure.

Maggie frowned, her curiosity pricked. In a place where sex was a common pastime, no one had any need to sneak around. It crossed Maggie's mind that making love in a wine cellar in the middle of the night might be one of her guest's most private fantasies, but instinct told her that this wasn't the case. If such a request had been made, the member of staff involved would have had to obtain the key from either Maggie or the cellar-man. Either way she would have known about it.

The woman moaned again, a low, drawn-out keening sound that made the hairs stand up at the back of Maggie's neck.

'Ooh! Yes, again, aah!'

Maggie swallowed, hard, aware that her body had responded to the moans of pleasure by growing warm and heavy. A dull pulse began to beat between her

74

legs, low and insistent. Slipping off her shoes so as not to alert the lovers to her presence, she tiptoed down the stone steps.

She saw the woman first, her face illuminated by the dull glow of the old hurricane lamp which was kept on the wall. For a second she did not recognise Gina, the receptionist who had been on duty the night before. Her face was distorted in a rictus of ecstasy, her soft lips pulled wide over her teeth, her eyes glazed, her pale skin flushed rosily.

Her back was against the stone wall, her skirt rucked up, over her stomach, her bare legs wrapped around the waist of a man wearing leather trousers and heavy, calf-length black boots, crisscrossed by straps fastened with silver buckles. The kind of boots worn by motorcyclists.

Maggie drew in her breath as she realised who it was. His long, black hair was loose, rippling down his back in a shiny curtain, obscuring his face as he bent his lips to the exposed curve of Gina's throat. He must have simply unzipped his trousers to release his cock, for it was quite obvious to Maggie that it was buried inside Gina and that he was thrusting as far as he was able, back and forth, supporting them both with a wide-legged stance. The beginning of the shadowed crease between his buttocks was just visible above the black leather, enough to demonstrate that he had an all-over tan and an economical sexual style that made Maggie's throat ache with lust.

Her first instinct was to step forward and demand to know what he thought he was doing on her property, but, apart from an awareness that the question would make her appear extremely foolish, Maggie didn't want to interrupt them. Though she hated to admit it, even to herself, the sight of the biker making love to Gina excited her, making her want to see the episode through to its inevitable conclusion.

Drawing back into the shadows, she watched as Gina let her head fall back on her shoulders, a dull flush spreading up from her chest into her neck and face.

'Uhh – that's so-o good,' she groaned, allowing her eyes to flutter to a close.

The biker chuckled, grinding his hips against hers in such a way that made her cry out, her arms grasping at his leather covered buttocks and pressing him harder against her.

'You bastard,' she hissed, all trace of the uncertain, shy receptionist Maggie knew swept away on a tide of lust. 'Go on then – harder.'

Maggie's eyes widened as she saw his hips buck faster, while Gina urged him on with increasingly outrageous obsenities.

'Wild cat,' he growled.

Reaching into the bodice of her dress, he scooped her breasts from their lacy bra cups and shoved them together, pressing her nipples with his thumbs.

'Oh yes. Suck them. Suck my tits!'

The biker obliged, moving his mouth from one to the other, drawing the quivering flesh in and sucking her nipples into hard, shiny cones. Gina was panting, her head moving from side to side, her thighs pressed tight around his waist.

Suddenly, he reached down, placing his hands on her wide-spread buttocks, his fingers splayed out. With a grunt which sent shivers up Maggie's spine, he twisted his hips to increase his penetration.

Gina squealed, her heels battering against his buttocks as she came, forcing him in still deeper. He

76

shuddered, uttering a deep, masculine groan which sent a fresh rush of moisture to the soft folds of flesh between Maggie's thighs.

It was then that Gina opened her eyes – and locked her gaze with Maggie's. Shock chased the post-coital glaze from her eyes and they opened wide with alarm.

'Maggie, oh my God!' she said, detaching herself from the biker with an inelegant tug.

Maggie struggled to recover her own equilibrium sufficiently to adopt a suitably employer-like outrage.

'Just *what* do you think you are doing?' she asked frostily.

Gina's cheeks flamed as she straightened her clothing, her eyes sliding away from Maggie's.

'I – I mean, we – um . . .'

'I think we were fucking.'

Both women turned their attention to the biker. He was looking straight at Maggie, a mocking expression in his hard blue eyes which started a wholly inappropriate churning in the pit of her stomach. She had the feeling that he could see right through her, that he knew she had been aroused by watching them and was trying hard to disguise it.

Her eyes slid to his fingers which were re-fastening his leather jeans, tucking in his shirt, which was white and none too clean, she couldn't help noting. There was an arrogance in his actions, an insouciance which, though she guessed he meant it to annoy her, actually had the opposite effect, making her even more intrigued by him.

Keeping her expression haughty, Maggie forced her eyes away from him and onto the hapless girl who was now visibly trembling.

'Who is this person, Gina?'

'Jake. Jake Curran. I'm sorry, Maggie, it won't happen again.'

Maggie took pity on her. If it had been anyone else she would have been indulgent, not censorious.

'It's all right, Gina – it's not as if you're on duty. I would like to know, though, whether this has happened before?'

The look on Gina's face was enough to signal her guilt.

'Last night?' Maggie suggested, her voice dangerously low.

'You know damn well I was here last night,' the biker interjected in his lazy drawl. There was amusement in his voice and Maggie felt her hackles rise. 'You saw me – remember?'

Recalling the sensation she had felt of being watched while she was making love with Antony, Maggie's eyes narrowed angrily.

'No, Mr Curran, I didn't. *You* saw *me* – isn't that right?'

His hard lips turned up slightly at the corners in what Maggie supposed passed for a smile. He neither confirmed nor denied her accusation, merely telling her: 'I'd say that makes us even.'

He seemed to be about to leave, but Gina grabbed at his arm. 'Where are you going, Jake?' she said, a note of panic entering her voice.

Jake Curran looked down at her hand on his arm and Gina abruptly withdrew it. There was a coldness in his eyes when he looked at the other girl which made Maggie feel indignant on her behalf.

'I'll see you around,' he said cruelly, turning away and brushing past Maggie on his way to the stairs.

Maggie closed her eyes briefly as he passed her. He smelled of axle grease, sweat and sex, a powerfully evocative combination. It took her a few seconds to register that he was already running up the stairs towards the courtyard. Forgetting about Gina staring disconsolately after him, Maggie followed.

'Wait, *Mr* Curran.'

He paused outside and turned to her, a quizzical expression playing around his eyes.

'You might have heard we had a fire in this building last night.'

He stared at her, incomprehension darkening his eyes. 'I heard. What of it?'

'The fire officer believes it could have been started deliberately,' she said pointedly. 'You wouldn't happen to know anything about that, would you?'

Incredulity was quickly chased away by disgust as he realised what she was implying. 'What makes you think I might?' he said, contempt colouring his every word.

'Do you?' Maggie asked, determined to stand her ground and challenge him.

He took a few seconds to reply, seconds in which Maggie found herself aware of the tension in him, the violence she sensed coiling within him making her heart beat faster. This man was dangerous, unpredictable. Maggie didn't like the fact that she found him sexy as hell, regardless.

'No, I don't, he told her, his eyes raking insolently over her body.

'The police might want you to confirm that to them,' she told him, watching him closely for any sign of guilt.

His lip curled derisively and she almost flinched under the weight of his contempt. 'Will they now?' he said. 'Well, you know where I'm moored, Maggie. I'm not planning on going anywhere.'

He turned and strode away, leaving Maggie staring after him with mixed feelings. She still sensed the danger in him, but she was aware that it was this that excited her. As on the first occasion when they had met, she was left with the feeling that he had bested her. It was not a feeling that she liked.

Gina joined her on the driveway and the two women watched in silence as Jake Curran roared away on his motorbike, spraying gravel in his wake.

'Bastard,' Gina commented without acrimony.

Maggie looked at her. After the sex was over, the biker had merely zipped himself up and walked away without a backward glance at Gina.

'Are you all right?' she asked.

Gina shot her a brief, self-deprecating smile. 'Yes. I'm sorry about that, Maggie.'

Maggie shrugged and, after locking the door to the cellar, began walking back to the hotel.

'It's okay. Your boyfriend didn't seem to be in the least bit fazed by my arrival.'

Gina laughed. 'I don't suppose he was. Jake Curran is the kind of man who writes his own rules.'

'Really? Have you known him for long?'

Gina, who had been born and brought up nearby, nodded her head. 'On and off. We went to school together, or rather, we were registered at the same time. Not that Jake ever bothered to go much.'

'What does he do for a living?'

Gina shrugged again. 'This and that, I suppose. Anything where he can use his bike and which won't tie him down.'

'Hmm. I know his sort,' Maggie remarked drily.

Gina grimaced. 'Like I said – he's a total bastard.'

'So?'

'So what?'

'So why do you see him?'

Gina grinned suddenly. 'Because though Jake Curran might be the devil incarnate, he fucks like an angel.'

Maggie had to force herself not to dwell on Gina's testimony, it only confirmed what she herself already expected.

'I see,' she said tightly.

Gina fidgeted, gaining her attention. 'Can I go now, Maggie?'

Maggie looked at her in surprise. From the way she had been talking, she hadn't realised that Gina felt she was being hauled over the coals.

'Of course,' she told her, adding as an afterthought, 'but I'd like you to be careful of that man. I don't think he's altogether to be trusted.'

Gina looked at her askance.

'I'm sorry,' Maggie said ruefully. 'It's late and I'm tired – I have no right to comment on your private affairs. It's not as if you're one of the waiting staff. You're not bound by the "no outside relationships" rule.'

Gina smiled. 'It's all right. And don't worry – I know how to handle Jake. The best thing is *not* to trust him in the first place, that way there's no chance of getting hurt. Goodnight.'

'Goodnight,' Maggie murmured, digesting this last homily.

She had been honest when she told Gina she was tired. Wearily, she trudged up the stairs, forcing all thoughts of Jake Curran from her mind as she went to check on Lena.

Lena did not respond to her gentle knock on her door, so Maggie let herself in and softly called her name.

'Lena? It's Maggie. Are you all right?'

Tiptoeing over to the bed, she peered at the pale face which was turned away from her on the pillows.

'Lena?'

Reaching out her hand, she smoothed a strand of red-gold hair away from her cheek. Her skin was cool and soft beneath her fingertips and Maggie could not resist the urge to trail her fingers lightly down the side of her face before removing her hand.

Lena's eyes opened and, slowly, she turned her head. Maggie caught her breath as she saw the glitter of her jewel-bright eyes in the gloom. Desire kicked in her stomach and she felt her mouth go dry.

'Maggie,' Lena whispered, a smile curving at the corners of her mouth as she recognised her.

'How – how do you feel?' Maggie stammered, feeling uncharacteristically tongue-tied.

Lena's gaze was unwavering, frankly sexual.

'Lena – '

Maggie turned as the other girl slowly peeled back the bed covers and she realised that she was naked beneath them. In the silvery moonlight filtering through the thin cotton curtains, her pale skin shone with a ghostly glow, the tender creases below her small breasts shadowed, her waist sculpted by the contrast in light. Maggie's breath hurt in her chest as she ran her eyes slowly over Lena's naked body, lingering on the short, wiry red curls on her mons and the long sweep of her legs from hip to knee.

She could smell her perfume, a light floral scent, mingled with the unique odour of her skin. There was a sharp, unmistakable undernote of arousal. Maggie swallowed, hard. Her own sex flesh fluttered in response to the stimulus and her fingers itched to stroke the soft skin so boldly displayed on the bed in front of her. Still she held back, aware that they were teetering on the brink of something that would change the tenor of their relationship forever.

'Are you sure?' she whispered, watching Lena's face as she spoke.

Lena smiled, a wide, serene smile that seemed to light up her face from within. 'I've been waiting for you,' she whispered.

Slowly, she picked up Maggie's hand and placed it on her left breast, just above her heart. Maggie could feel the puckered nub of her nipple pressing into her palm, making it tingle.

'Can you feel my heart beating?' Lena asked her, her voice low and husky. 'It's racing – out of control.'

It was indeed beating very fast. Throwing off her hesitation, Maggie gave a small sigh and bent her head. Pressing her lips against the warmth of Lena's skin, just above her left nipple, she pushed the tip of her tongue between her lips and tasted the warm, slightly salty flesh

Lena sighed raggedly and began to stroke Maggie's hair. 'Your lips are so soft,' she whispered into the darkness. 'So soft.'

In response, Maggie brushed her mouth gently inward, kissing and licking a path between Lena's small breasts and nuzzling the sensitive undersides. The soft breast flesh quivered, the nipples rising and cresting as Maggie stroked them gently with her fingertips while her lips moved slowly downward towards her navel.

Lena's belly was taut with anticipation as Maggie circled it with little kisses, working inwards towards the dip of her navel. She could smell the perfume of her arousal, could see the glistening pink folds of flesh which nestled between the other girl's legs as she allowed her thighs to fall softly apart.

Maggie's lips curved against her skin and she raised herself up so that she could see Lena's face. Standing, she undressed quickly, her eyes never leaving Lena's. The first contact of the air against her skin made her shiver, her flesh rising in small goosebumps. Noticing, Lena held back the covers in an unspoken invitation to join her in the bed.

Slipping between the sheets, Maggie rolled onto her side, her breasts brushing against Lena's as she turned into her arms. Facing each other, they kissed, tentatively at first, then more hungrily, their tongues parrying as they pressed their lips closer together. Maggie liked the taste of Lena's lips; they were sweet and soft, deliciously feminine as they opened under hers.

Lena's arms came around her, pressing her close. Returning the embrace, Maggie revelled in the silky slip of soft skin against hers. The erectile tissue of Lena's nipples pressed urgently against hers, almost abrasive in the way that they brushed back and forth over the surface as Lena moved. Maggie could feel the heat of her sex burning like a furnace against the shaven skin of her own mons and she moaned softly.

'Sweet Lena,' she whispered, running her fingers through the other girl's hair.

'I never thought this time would come,' Lena said, her voice trembling with emotion. 'I love you, Maggie.'

Before Maggie could react, she slipped down the bed and pressed her lips against the cleft of her vulva. Maggie felt a fluttering start deep in her womb and allowed her legs to part, offering access to Lena's burrowing tongue. She groaned, arching her back and tipping her pelvis upward as Lena's warm, wet tongue probed the moistening channels of her sex.

Oral sex with a woman was always exciting, for only another woman could really know how it felt. Lena was demonstrating this fact even as Maggie thought it, nibbling at her labia with her lips, folding them back with the flat of her tongue before using the tip to coax her clitoris from beneath its protective hood.

It hardened at once, thrusting itself towards Lena's mouth, anticipating the stab of her tongue on its tip. She did not disappoint, moving the hard little bud against the underlying pelvic bone, back and forth until Maggie felt the sweat break out on her skin. She moved restlessly, her legs widening, her body admitting first one, then two fingers which Lena moved slowly in and out of her.

Crooking her fingers, she found the sensitive spot deep inside the elastic walls of Maggie's vagina, and pressed against her pubic bone from within. At the same time, she flicked her clitoris with her tongue, back and forth with ever-increasing rhythm until Maggie's hips bucked and she came, crying out softly as Lena kept the sensations going for what seemed like an age.

Sliding back up the bed, Lena smiled triumphantly at Maggie, her eyes glittering at her in the gloom.

'You taste good,' she whispered. 'Here – '

She thrust her tongue back between Maggie's lips so that she could taste her own secretions on Lena's lips and tongue. They kissed, deeply, as Maggie's hands roamed the other woman's body, discovering its shape and texture. Lena sighed and lay back, closing her eyes as Maggie slipped her fingers between her legs and began to stroke her.

Maggie watched Lena's face as she moved her fingers across the moisture-slick skin of her sex. Using her thumb, she circled the hard bead of her clitoris, bringing the moisture from the lip of her vagina with her middle finger to coat it and make her progress easier.

A frown of concentration was etched between the other woman's finely drawn eyebrows as Maggie increased the tempo of her movements.

'Push it out for me, Lena,' she whispered as she sensed that the other girl was finding it difficult to let go. 'That's it – harder. Give it to me . . .'

Maggie felt the pulsing in the tiny bundle of nerve endings and knew that Lena was falling over the edge. She shuddered from head to toe as she lost control and her orgasm rippled through her, gently at first, then spiralling, out of control, the strength of it clearly taking her by surprise.

Stretching out her legs, Lena pointed her toes to prolong the sensation for as long as possible, then she scissored them, effectively trapping Maggie's hand between her thighs. Maggie curled her fingers into the pulpy, convulsing flesh, squeezing gently to help her eke out every last drop of feeling.

Opening her eyes, Lena smiled at her. 'Oh, Maggie.'

Able at last to withdraw her hand, Maggie cupped the other girl's face and kissed her, tenderly, on the lips.

'Will you sleep with me tonight?' Lena whispered when they finally broke apart.

Maggie hesitated, aware that she was on dangerous ground, spending the night with one of her employees. Then she smiled. She was the boss, after all, and one of the perks of the job had to be that she could chop and change the rules to suit herself on occasion.

'All right,' she agreed, stroking Lena's face. 'But only because I want to make sure you sleep well.'

Lena grinned happily. 'Sleep?' she retorted. 'I don't want to sleep at all.'

She cupped Maggie's vulva with one hand and began to stroke the shaven skin, smoothing it downward in the direction that her pubic hair would grow.

'I like this,' she said after a minute or two. 'It leaves everything on show, available.'

Maggie raised her eyebrows. 'That's the idea. To mark me as available.'

Lena stiffened slightly. 'Available for Alexander?'

Not missing the note of possessiveness which coloured Lena's tone, Maggie chose to ignore it. 'Yes. It's like a mark of ownership, of belonging. Rather like my tattoo.'

Lena's face brightened. 'The black orchid? Can I see it?'

Maggie rolled onto her side, presenting Lena with a view of her back. Wriggling up the bed, she reached behind herself and pulled her buttocks apart to reveal the motif tattooed on the tender area between her bottom and the top of her thigh.

'Do you see it?'

Lena traced the little black orchid with the tip of her finger. 'It's beautiful,' she murmured.

Maggie sensed that she was talking about more than the tattoo and she shivered as Lena caressed the sensitive crease between her buttocks.

'Lena – '

'I'd like one of these,' Lena interrupted her. 'Or some other sign to show the world that I belong to you.'

Maggie felt a small prick of apprehension at the fervently uttered words, but she soon forgot them as

87

Lena suddenly, unexpectedly, pressed the sharp tip of her tongue against the puckered areola surrounding her anus.

'Oh God,' she groaned as, making a point with her tongue, Lena rimmed the entrance, jabbing at the forbidden orifice until Maggie felt her sex flesh swell and moisten once more.

Lena replaced her tongue with her finger and entered her gently, reaching out with her other hand to fondle Maggie's breasts.

'I love you, Maggie,' she whispered, her breath hot against Maggie's ear. 'I love you.'

Chapter Six

*A*s the gentle, pinkish light of dawn filtered through the curtains, Maggie lay, wakeful, listening to the even breathing of the girl beside her. So much seemed to have happened in the past few days – encountering Jake Curran, the fire, embarking on this affair with Lena – Maggie felt exhausted. She could hardly continue to complain that her life had become monotonous.

She and Lena had made love again before they slept, moving together breast to breast, pelvis to pelvis, until Lena had urged her to lie still while she manoeuvred herself so that they were lying top to toe in a sixty-nine. Maggie could even now faintly taste the other girl on her tongue, could still feel the pleasurable ache in the folds of her vulva where Lena had used her lips and tongue to bring her to one climax after another.

Without doubt, it had been a deeply satisfying night. And and emotional one, for Maggie had felt a kinship with the other girl which only served to make the sex more erotic, more desirable. So why was she left with a feeling of such marked unease?

Shifting uncomfortably on to her side, Maggie watched the other girl's face. Lena's features were softer in sleep, more vulnerable. The fine down which grew on her freckled skin was highlighted by a shaft of early morning sun. Propping herself on one elbow, Maggie reached out and traced its path down her back with her fingertip. Lena murmured softly, but did not wake.

I love you, Maggie, I love you so much. The words echoed in Maggie's head, like a warning. There had been something quite desperate in the repeated declaration, something which sent a shiver of alarm along Maggie's spine. Instinct told her that this was no surface endearment uttered in the extremes of passion, and she wondered how long Lena had harboured such thoughts about her. Part of her was flattered, another part felt trapped, panicky, out of control.

Slowly, she became aware that Lena had opened her eyes and was looking steadily at her. Maggie's lips curved in a smile.

'Good morning,' she whispered, trailing her fingertips lightly over Lena's slightly parted lips. 'How are you feeling today?'

Lena stared up at her, her eyes huge in the half light. 'G-good morning,' she stammered. 'Maggie, you don't – you don't regret last night, do you?'

There was such an earnestness in the other girl's gaze, such trust in the way she was looking at her, that Maggie instantly felt guilty for her treacherous thoughts of mere seconds before.

'Of course not,' she assured her quickly. 'How could I regret it?'

Lena's expression cleared a little, but a trace of anxiety remained in her eyes. 'You won't leave me now Maggie, will you?'

Maggie frowned, wondering what was expected of her. 'Leave you? What do you mean?'

Slowly, Lena reached up and stroked the curve of Maggie's cheek with her fingertips. 'You're so beautiful,' she whispered. 'So perfect. I love you.'

She snatched her hand back as Maggie was unable to suppress a frown. 'Don't you love me?'

Her tone held a petulance which grated on Maggie's nerves, but still she sought to be gentle. 'Of course I do,' she said lightly. 'How could we have shared what we shared last night without there being love between us?'

Pain flitted across Lena's features, so fleeting that Maggie thought at first she might have imagined it. Then she spoke and she knew that it had been real.

'Are you in love with Antony?'

'I'm connected to Antony. I love him dearly.'

'And Alexander?'

Maggie smiled and shook her head. Laying back on the pillows, she stared up at the ceiling, watching the shadows flutter across the surface. 'Ah, Alexander. He's different.'

Lena raised herself up on one elbow so that their positions were reversed and she was staring down at Maggie. 'In what way different?' she asked.

Maggie shrugged her shoulders slightly. 'I can't explain. You wouldn't understand. Sometimes I wonder if I understand myself.'

'But do you love him?' Lena pressed her.

Maggie frowned, irritated by the other girl's persistence. 'I don't know. Why are you so hung up on love?

91

Isn't it enough that two people can each find pleasure in the other, as we did last night?'

Lena's expression darkened. 'Is that all it meant to you? Am I just a cheap lay, soon forgotten?'

'Of course not. You know I don't think of you like that, Lena.'

'Do I?' Lena's eyes flickered away from Maggie's for a moment before fastening on hers again, even more fiercely than before. 'What did last night mean to you, Maggie?'

Maggie regarded her warily. 'What did it mean to you?' she asked cautiously.

'I love you,' Lena said, her voice low and urgent. 'I love you, Maggie, with all my heart and soul. I want you to love me like that, I want you to love me back.'

Maggie took several minutes to gather her thoughts before she replied. At last, she sat up and, pulling the duvet up around her shoulders, she faced the other girl squarely. 'Lena, I've told you that I love you, but I don't think that when I say those words and when you say them we're both talking about the same thing.' She paused, aware that Lena was staring at her intently, her arms clasped tightly around her knees as she listened. She flinched away when Maggie tried to touch her face and Maggie sighed.

'I think you want me to love you exclusively – is that right?' Lena didn't answer, merely stared fixedly at Maggie. 'I don't want to hurt you, Lena – but if that is the case then you have to understand that I can't give you what you want.'

'How can you say that?' Lena suddenly burst out passionately. 'Why won't you give us a chance?'

Maggie looked at her, trying to hide her dismay. How could she had misread Lena's needs so comprehensively?

'Lena – you know me! I'm just not the monogamous type.' she protested. 'Come here . . .'

Putting her arms around Lena's shoulders, she cuddled her for a moment, aware as she did so that the other girl was struggling to bring herself under control.

After a few minutes, Lena ventured, 'I understand what you're saying, Maggie. Truly I do. But, don't you think you'd settle down and be faithful if you found the right person?'

Maggie felt a pang as she realised that Lena was hopeful that the 'right person' of whom she spoke might be her. 'No,' she said, aware that there was no gentle way to let the girl down. 'I'm sorry. I had no idea you felt like this.'

Lena was quiet for a few moments. Then she raised her face to Maggie's and smiled. 'It's all right,' she said brightly. 'I don't mind, really I don't. I know you like to sleep with other people. I can live with that. But you'll love me best, I know you will.'

With that, she smiled serenely and kissed Maggie on the mouth. Maggie remained passive, her brain racing. Hadn't Lena understood what she was trying to say?

'Lena – '

'Ssh!' Lena put her fingertip against Maggie's lips. 'Don't say anything. We don't need words, Maggie. We don't need anything but this . . .'

And with that she pressed her lips against Maggie's, effectively silencing her. It didn't matter, Maggie told herself as she allowed herself to be seduced again. Lena was merely over-reacting to the excessive emotion caused by a night of fairly mind-blowing sex. She would soon forget her need for exclusivity, Maggie had only to continue to live as she had always lived. Lena would soon see she could not shackle her and would turn her attention elsewhere. It would be all right.

Meanwhile, she was doing something rather interesting with her fingers in the region of Maggie's vulva, and after a few more moments Maggie ceased to think rationally at all.

Maggie was on duty when Brett Tunnock, the fire officer who had attended the night before, turned up for the promised inspection. Now here was a potent argument for bisexuality, Maggie told herself as she followed him around the building, paying more attention to his nicely muscled buttocks than to his occasional attempts at small talk. Making love to other women was all very well, but she would never want to give up the singular pleasure of a hard male body entering hers.

Brett Tunnock was a fine specimen, she saw now. Probably in his mid to late-forties his thick, dark hair was greying at the temples and he had the kind of face which reflected his personality. The network of lines around his eyes and at the corners of his mouth were arranged in such a way that suggested he was a man who liked to laugh. There was a lively intelligence in his deep-blue eyes and a fullness to his lower lip which held a wealth of sensual promise.

Underneath the bulky uniform he had worn the night before was a well-toned body, shown to pleasant advantage in his pristine white shirt and tailored trousers. Obviously, his job kept him in trim, but a man of his age would have to work hard to maintain such a physique and Maggie was impressed by the evidence of such self-discipline.

'Well?' she asked him when they had completed

their tour, finishing up, at her suggestion, in Maggie's office. 'Do we pass muster?'

Brett sat in the chair she had indicated, looking completely at ease. 'I'll send you a copy of my report,' he replied. 'Meanwhile, the police will want to interview everyone who was at the hotel last night.'

'Really? Is that absolutely necessary?' Maggie said, her heart sinking at the thought of her clients' reaction to being told they were under investigation. After all, the activities on offer at the Black Orchid Hotel were nothing if not secret. And if the press should get hold of the story . . . Maggie suppressed a shudder.

'I'm afraid so,' Brett said coolly. 'Procedure.'

Maggie smiled politely at him and offered him coffee. She could not help but notice that his eyes followed the movement of her legs as she sat down opposite him, and she crossed one over the other slowly, displaying them to advantage in her short skirt.

'Have you been in the fire service long . . . Brett?' she asked, allowing her voice to drop huskily on his name.

'Fifteen years. And you, Maggie – how long have you been in the hotel trade?'

Maggie suppressed a smile at his assessment of her job. 'Not long at all. I like to keep a little variety in my life. I'm easily bored.'

Brett narrowed his eyes and Maggie knew that he had not missed her *double entendre*. Though all her instincts urged her to take things a step further, she waited, judging that he was the kind of man who would want to feel as if he had made all the moves. He did not disappoint her. Leaning forward, he fixed her with a frank gaze, his lips curving slightly into a smile.

'What bores you, Maggie?' he asked, his eyes twinkling with amusement.

'Oh, you know,' she replied airily, 'the usual things. Routine. Commitment. Lack of imagination . . .' she paused to enjoy the expression in his eyes.

At that moment the coffee arrived and Maggie smiled at Susie, the new 'waitress', who brought it in. The girl kept glancing at Brett as she walked across the room. Laying the silver tray on the coffee table between them, she leaned towards him giving a view of her pert breasts, but Brett didn't notice her, his eyes were firmly clamped on Maggie.

Susie retreated with a small shrug of her narrow shoulders and Maggie made a mental note to advise the girl that the idea was not so much to offer herself at every available opportunity, but to try to second guess the needs of the guests. The fact that the handsome fire officer wasn't even a guest at the hotel was another point against her.

Maggie smiled slightly as Susie left them, knowing that the girl was more than capable of engineering such an indiscretion just so that Maggie would punish her. Perhaps she would, Maggie mused, filing the incident away for future reference. There was bound to be an opportunity to educate the girl whilst at the same time fulfilling a guest's fantasy. There usually was.

'You seem very distracted suddenly.'

Maggie pulled her attention back to the man in front of her and lifted the coffee cup to her lips before replying. The hot liquid was strong and bitter, just as she liked it. Putting the cup carefully back on its saucer, she looked Brett Tunnock straight in the eye.

'I was wondering if you might like to join me for lunch?'

For a moment Maggie thought she had gone too far too fast; Brett sat back in his seat and regarded her through narrowed eyes. Then he smiled, flashing white, even teeth at her.

'That's very hospitable of you,' he said, rising slowly to his feet.

Maggie stood up and moved round the coffee table until she was standing toe to toe with him. They weren't touching, yet she could feel the healthy, animal warmth of his body reaching out to her. The perfume of his aftershave was light and understated, allowing the scent of man to predominate. Maggie flared her nostrils, enjoying this first contact of their senses.

Brett's eyes ran unhurriedly across her face and down the front of her body. Maggie had the feeling that he too was enjoying the subtle sensuality of his first sensory contact with her. Instinct told her that he would be the kind of lover who liked to take his time, to relish each and every experience to the utmost without feeling the need to rush. Anticipation made her skin tingle and her secret flesh swell and moisten.

Slowly, very slowly, Brett reached for her. His strong, square-tipped fingers cupped her cheek and slid behind her head to the nape of her neck. Maggie stood absolutely still, enjoying the exquisite tension of waiting for his lips to touch hers.

His hand was warm at the base of her skull, the skin slightly rough against the softness of hers. Maggie felt her stomach tighten, her breasts hardening as they strained towards him. His eyes were on her lips now, caressing them, as if imagining how they would feel and taste. Just as Maggie thought he would never kiss her, he lowered his head and brushed the sensitive surface of her lower lip with his

97

before pressing a small, closed-mouth kiss at the corner of her mouth.

Maggie sighed, her lips parting slightly as his warm breath tickled over the surface. Again he brushed her lower lip, this time with his top one, before pressing gently at the centre with his thumb, exposing the sensitive inner surface. His tongue probed lightly at the tender skin as his free arm came around Maggie's waist, pressing her to him.

Reaching her arms up, around his neck, Maggie gave in to the overwhelming urge to sway towards him. As she had expected, his body was hard and unyielding, forcing her softer curves to mould themselves against him. She felt weak at the knees, more so as he began to kiss her properly, his tongue seeking access to her mouth, his lips closing over hers.

It was the most erotic kiss Maggie had enjoyed for a long, long time and she found herself clinging to him, not wanting it to end. When, at last, they broke apart, she saw her own excitement reflected in his eyes and knew that Brett was as overwhelmed by this first contact between them as she was.

To her relief, he resumed kissing her at once, his fingers working on the tense muscle at the top of her neck, kneading and squeezing until she felt she would dissolve with the pleasure of it. At first she had planned to invite him back for dinner another night, assuming that he would be the kind of man who would appreciate the chase, but now she wanted him with such urgency she knew she lacked the self-discipline to stick to her original strategy. As soon as he came up for air again, she would suggest that they lock the office door and . . .

Maggie started as a discordant electronic bleeper sounded from somewhere in the region of his trouser pocket. A cold waft of air came between them as he pulled away, shooting her a rueful grimace as he took out the bleeper and switched it off.

'Do you have a phone I could use?'

'Be my guest.'

Maggie stood back as he went to the telephone on her desk. Without the heat of his body she felt unnaturally cold and she shivered, folding her arms around herself. Watching Brett's face as he spoke, she knew he was going to have to leave.

'I'm sorry,' he said, reaching for his jacket and making for the door. 'Another time?'

Maggie shrugged, disappointment making her stomach churn. Brett crossed the room and pulled her into his arms for one last, hard kiss.

'When I'm off duty – when we can take things slowly. He ran the tip of his forefinger from her lips, down her throat to her cleavage. 'All right?'

Maggie nodded, unable to speak for her mouth and throat had dried and it had become inexplicably hard to breathe. Brett smiled, a wholly masculine, knowing smile which made her feel weak, then he turned on his heel and was gone, leaving Maggie staring after him.

'Who was that?'

Maggie pulled herself together with an effort as Lena came into the room a few minutes later.

'Lena! Should you be up and about yet?'

Aware that her face was flushed and her lips swollen after their prolonged contact with Brett's, Maggie turned away and shuffled some papers on her desk. Lena walked to a spot where she could see her face and stared at her accusingly.

'I feel all right. You didn't tell me you were interviewing today.'

99

'I wasn't. That was Brett Tunnock, the local fire officer. He's just completed his inspection.'

'I hadn't realised you were a fire hazard.'

'Lena,' Maggie felt the anger rise as she faced her assistant. This was going to have to stop before it got out of hand. 'What I do in my own office is nobody's concern but my own. You don't own me Lena. Do you understand?'

Lena looked at her with horror for a moment, then her face crumpled and, to Maggie's dismay, she began to cry. Not quietly, but with great, gulping sobs which she muffled by hiding her face in her hands. Alarmed, Maggie rushed to her side and guided her to a chair.

'Lena – don't. Are you ill?'

The girl shook her head and Maggie smoothed her soft, red hair away from her face.

'Please don't cry. You're overwrought – go back to bed.'

Lena caught at her arm. 'I'm sorry, Maggie,' she gulped. 'Please, please don't think badly of me. I don't mind what you do, honestly I don't.'

Feeling uncomfortable, Maggie dropped to her knees and cradled Lena's head on her shoulder. 'You mustn't see it as a slur on you,' she muttered awkwardly.

'It doesn't matter, really it doesn't. I know you love me best. You do, don't you Maggie? You do love me best?'

Maggie stared down into Lena's wild eyes and wondered if she might be running a temperature. She was certainly hot and flushed and her questions were feverish, her grip on her arm desperate. It might be best to humour her – anything to persuade her back to bed.

100

'Of course.' She smiled reassuringly. 'Of course I do. Come on now – let's get you back upstairs.'

But Lena was not satisfied. 'Say you love me, Maggie. Please?'

Maggie opened her mouth to protest, but one glance at the other girl's pleading eyes made her relent. 'I love you, Lena. There – satisfied?'

Lena stared at her for several seconds, as if trying to gauge her sincerity. Then an angelic smile spread across her features and her eyes sparkled with tears of happiness instead of distress.

'Oh Maggie,' she cried, throwing her arms around Maggie's neck and hugging her. 'I knew you did, I knew you loved me best.'

'Of course,' Maggie murmured, coaxing the other girl to her feet. 'Now please get some rest.'

This time Lena did not resist as Maggie steered her towards the door, though there was no way she would let go of Maggie's arm and so she was forced to settle her once more in her bedroom before she could escape.

Unnerved by the incident with Lena, and still frustrated by the abrupt termination of her encounter with Brett, Maggie decided to take the afternoon off and get out of the hotel for a few hours. On an impulse, she left her mobile phone behind so that no one could bother her.

It was a beautiful day. Cotton-wool clouds drifted lazily across a sapphire-blue sky and the sun shone with a gentle, benign warmth. Maggie rolled down the top of her cabriolet and put her foot down as she drew out of the hotel driveway. With the wind whipping through her hair and Robert Plant playing at full blast on the CD player, Maggie allowed her mind to clear and her spirits to lift.

Her sense of well-being persisted after a good afternoon's shopping. Stacking her carrier bags in the boot she decided to take the winding, little-used country roads back to the hotel. Driving more slowly than usual so that she could admire the view, it was almost half an hour before she passed the tiny village that she always considered to be the halfway point between the hotel and the town.

Suddenly, the car began to lose power. Cursing under her breath, Maggie freewheeled to the side of the road and turned off the ignition. After a few minutes, she turned the key again, wincing as she was rewarded by a very sick-sounding grating noise.

Car maintenance had never been of particular interest to her, but she had made sure that she knew the basics, at least enough to get by. Now as she raised the bonnet and peered inside, her heart sank. Trying to disregard her beautifully manicured nails, she began the laborious process of checking each part of the engine.

Fifteen minutes later she stood back and passed an oily hand over her forehead. It was clear that the car wasn't going to get her anywhere and she was stranded – miles from anywhere, wearing spike-heeled sandals and without her mobile phone. That would teach her to skive off by herself for a whole afternoon, she thought wryly.

Maggie looked up expectantly as the distant sound of an engine disturbed the peace. It came closer and she held her breath, willing whoever it was to take the side road where she was stranded and not turn off onto the main carriageway. Luck was on her side and she straightened, ready to flag down the approaching motorist and beg a lift to the nearest telephone.

As she took up position in the centre of the road, Maggie saw, in the distance, that it was not a car at all, but a motorbike. A motorbike which she recognised.

For one frantic second, she considered clambering over into a neighbouring field so that it would look as though she had already abandoned her car. But Jake Curran was approaching fast, chances were he would pass just as she was straddling the thorny hedge and then she would feel, and look, like a total fool. So, gritting her teeth, Maggie stood her ground and waited for him to notice her. He did, but not until he was almost on top of her, and she felt compelled to jump back out of his way.

'Problems?' he asked as the roar of his engine was finally stilled.

Maggie forced a tight smile. 'Yes, I think – '

'I'll have a look.'

Maggie seethed silently as he interrupted her and climbed calmly off his bike. Did he think her a total bimbo?

'The timing chain's snapped – there's nothing to be done,' she said as he approached the car.

Jake took off his helmet and his long, dark hair tumbled round his face. He was wearing old, frayed jeans which were none too clean and a faded red T-shirt which clung to his torso like a second skin. There was a large vee of sweat-darkened fabric between his pectorals and his bare forearms glistened beneath the dark hairs.

Pushing his hair back with one hand, he made an impatient gesture with the other. 'Are you sure?'

He was bending over the engine before Maggie had

a chance to reply and she bit back the sarcastic retort she could feel bubbling on her lips.

'Well?' she asked with acid sweetness as he straightened.

Jake flashed her a look and she saw that he was surprised. She was glad.

'You could be right,' he conceded grudgingly, delving back into the engine with a thoughtful frown.

'If you'd be good enough to run me home I'll gladly refund your petrol,' she suggested, growing impatient.

Jake shot her a contemptuous glance as he lowered the bonnet. 'Home?'

Maggie nodded. 'If it's not too much trouble.'

Jake's eyes travelled uncomfortably slowly over her white blouse and downward, his gaze lingering on the length of bare brown leg which emerged from her short red skirt. Maggie felt herself trembling and brought herself up angrily – she *would not* allow herself to be aroused by this uncouth lout. Nevertheless, his protracted scrutiny of her had the unfortunate effect of making her feel tense and her voice betrayed her agitation as she spoke.

'Well?'

Jake smiled at her and she knew that he was perfectly well aware of the effect he was having on her, and worse, that he was amused by it.

'There's a spare helmet in the box,' he told her, nodding towards the bike.

Gathering her dignity about her, Maggie secured her car and went to take the helmet which by now Jake had taken out of the box for her. Their fingertips met and she had to concentrate to conceal the shiver which went through her at his touch.

What was it about this man? He was the antithesis

of everything she looked for in a partner. Rough and surly, he had no manners, sexual or otherwise. He should have revolted her with his unkempt hair and his grubby jeans, and yet there was a raw sexuality about him which shone through the surface dishevelment and reached out to her. She hadn't needed Gina to tell her that he was a good lover – Maggie could sense it. It rose up from his pores like a miasma. He reeked of sex.

Maggie's hands shook as she fastened the strap of the crash helmet under her chin. With an impatient curse, Jake pushed her fingers away and saw to it himself.

Maggie stood very still. His mouth was mere inches from hers and she could feel the faint sigh of his breath against her face. His fingers were impatient against her skin and did not linger once the job was done, yet she imagined she could still feel them there as she climbed on to the pillion behind him.

The bike was large and powerful, stretching her thighs wide apart as she leaned forward to hold him round the waist. There wasn't a spare ounce of flesh on him, all that she could feel beneath her fingers was hard, unyielding muscle.

As he fired the engine, Maggie felt the power of the bike reverberate through her body and she clung to him more tightly as they drew away. The force of movement pushed her open crotch hard against the spread of his buttocks and Maggie felt a slow pulse begin to beat between her legs. Pressing her cheek into the damp dip between his shoulder-blades, she tried to catch her breath, half-terrified and half-exhilarated by the speed.

Aware that her skirt had ridden up to reveal her plain white panties, Maggie did not dare to try to tug it down, merely thanking providence that she had thought to put on underwear before leaving the hotel. Her eyes smarted, watering in the visorless helmet so that she could not see where she was going. The sound of the engine and the roar of the wind past her face rendered her deaf and blind, all her senses seemed concentrated on the places where their bodies touched: cheek to back, arms to waist, inner thighs to denim-clad buttocks.

For a few moments after they stopped, Maggie felt disorientated. She almost lost her balance as Jake climbed off the bike, robbing her of her support. Aware that she was sitting, legs splayed lewdly apart, in full view of anyone who might be passing, not to mention the disagreeable young man who had brought her home, she swung one leg awkwardly over the bike and stood shakily, smoothing her skirt over her bottom.

Only gradually did she realise that, far from standing on the familiar gravel of the hotel driveway, her heels were sinking into soft earth. Her mouth dropped open as her ears adjusted to the sound of the water and her eyes focused on the houseboat moored at the side of the estuary.

'What the hell are we doing here?' she said, turning on Jake Curran with blazing eyes.

He shrugged, totally unfazed, it seemed, by her fury. 'You asked me to take you home.' He gestured towards the houseboat. 'This is home.'

'*My* home, you – you Neanderthal idiot. What the hell makes you think I'd want to come here with you?'

Jake's eyes darkened and Maggie took a step back as he approached her. Had she gone too far? Glancing about her frantically, Maggie saw that they were completely alone on the bank of the estuary; no one would hear her if she had cause to cry out.

Her heel skewed in the soft mud and she would have fallen but for his hand shooting out to steady her. He held her wrist in a vice-like grip and pulled her towards him.

'We could fuck,' he said crudely.

Maggie's eyes widened and she frowned, offended by his approach. 'And pigs might fly,' she retorted, trying to pull away.

Jake would not allow her to move, his grip merely tightened and his lips curved into a smile that made little shivers of alarm run along her spine.

'Don't pretend you don't want it,' he said, his voice low and dangerous.

Maggie sneered bravely at him. 'Christ, you're unbelievable. I've never met a man who truly believed that all women are asking for it – '

'Not *all* women,' he interrupted her, pulling her close so that she could feel the heat of his body against the length of hers. 'Just you. You've wanted me since the first moment you set eyes on me.'

Maggie was outraged, yet a guilty voice in the back of her mind told her that he was right – she *did* want him. Was she that obvious?

Jake must have been able to read her mind, for he smiled and pushed her back so that the back of her legs were pressing against the parked motorbike. Overbalancing, Maggie's bottom came into contact with the wide leather seat and she fell back, on to her elbows.

Staring up at Jake, legs akimbo, her blouse gaping open and her skirt stretched across her open thighs, Maggie felt a sudden, almost violent rush of lust that made her head swim. Her breath caught in her chest and she was supremely conscious of her sex flesh swelling and moistening as Jake feasted his eyes on her.

'You're a hot little bitch,' he said quietly.

For some reason that remark struck Maggie as extraordinarily funny and she threw back her head and laughed. Catching Jake's eye, she saw the amusement sparking in the depths of his hard blue eyes and any trace of fear he might have invoked disappeared as if it had never come between them.

They had nothing in common at all. No interests, no friends, no values. All there was between them was sex – dark, dangerous, explosive. Thinking this, Maggie almost pulled back. Then he began to unbutton his jeans, and she knew that it was enough.

Chapter Seven

Jake held Maggie's eye as he eased each button through its buttonhole, his unfathomable blue eyes searching hers, as if half expecting her to back out. Maggie tried to hold his gaze but, conscious that he was peeling back the two sides of his fly, she could not help herself from looking down to where his cock, unhampered by underwear, reared up from his groin.

It was long and thick, the velvet-smooth, circumcised tip pointing straight at her. Maggie licked her dry lips with the tip of her tongue and shifted her bottom further back onto the motorbike so that she was lying, as far as she was able, crossways over the seat.

Jake moved closer and the tip of his penis bumped against the soft skin of her inner thigh as he leaned over her. His breath was hot against her cheek as he caught one earlobe between his teeth and bit gently on it, just hard enough to make her catch her breath.

The heat of him smothered her, yet they barely touched until he began to stroke one breast through the thin fabric of her blouse. Maggie felt her nipple harden and swell beneath his palm and she gripped his T-shirt at the shoulders to stop herself from toppling backwards. His fingers were hard and determined, digging into the softness of her flesh almost painfully.

His perfunctory approach inflamed her, incited her to raise her hips to meet the unselfconscious rasp of his cock as it moved across her skin. Maggie gasped as he covered the mound of her pubis with one hand, his fingers pressing the cotton of her briefs into the wet channels of her sex, gauging the strength of her desire.

Curling his fingertips around the elastic rim, Jake pulled her panties to one side and slid himself effortlessly into the welcoming sheath of her body. His gaze was hot as it locked with hers, his pupils growing so that there was the smallest margin of blue around their edge.

Maggie found herself straining towards him, wanting to feel his mouth against hers, but he would not kiss her, holding her away so that he could watch her face as he fucked her. He did so economically, with firm, sure thrusts, his rhythm regular and determined. Maggie felt a sense of unreality descend, caused, she was sure, by Jake's detachment as he slowly, almost clinically, drew a response from her body.

Vaguely, she was aware of the vastness of the sky above her and of the heat of his skin beneath his T-shirt. A seagull wheeled overhead, its screams oddly discordant, as if coming from a long way off. Jake was breathing heavily and his face was gilded by perspiration. Yet his expression remained impassive, strangely impersonal as he thrust in and out of her body.

Normally Maggie would require a far higher level of involvement before she could come, but there was something perversely erotic about Jake's no-nonsense approach which made her body twitch and buzz as she neared climax. Pulling herself up slightly from the waist, she angled herself so that his marauding penis scraped deliciously across her clitoris with every inward stroke, doubling her pleasure.

Their lips almost touched, but not quite, their eyes locked in a silent game of control. The motorbike rocked precariously beneath them, yet Maggie barely noticed. All her concentration was fixed on Jake and the rhythm of his body moving in and out of hers.

Her orgasm took her by surprise, breaking over her so suddenly that she could not stop herself from crying out and clinging to him. She saw the gleam of triumph in his eyes, closely followed by ecstasy as the pulsing of the cleated walls of her vagina drew the seed from his body.

He arched his neck back and Maggie pressed the flat of her tongue against the straining tendons, tasting the salt on his skin. Scraping her teeth lightly down his throat she bit gently on his collarbone, feeling the low growl of masculine satisfaction reverberate through her lips and onto her tongue.

For a few minutes, Jake rested inside her, then he withdrew so abruptly that Maggie caught her breath. She readjusted her underwear and pulled down her skirt as he tucked his sated penis back into his jeans. Watching him covertly, through her lashes, Maggie saw how his hair fell across his face and longed to reach out and touch it. Somehow, though, she knew he would not tolerate such intimacy, so she merely waited, hoping that the encounter was not at an end.

Jake glowered at her as they faced one another,

striking a pose that made her think of a contemporary James Dean. Maggie stared back at him, sure that her continued desire for him was written clearly in her eyes. Her breasts heaved as she sought to bring her breathing under control and her heart raced in her chest as she waited for his next move.

'Get inside,' he said at last, jerking his head towards the houseboat.

Something about the timbre of his voice made Maggie feel as if she might come again, just through listening to it. It had been a long time, longer than she could remember, since a man had dared to treat her like this. Even with Alexander, though he had often treated her with something very close to cruelty, she always knew that he was merely playing with her, that he was acting a part.

Jake wasn't play-acting – he was a genuine rough diamond, and after the years of sophisticated sex she had enjoyed, Maggie found his approach extraordinarily exciting. Without a word, she turned and stepped onto the deck of the boat.

Inside the battered hatch, Maggue found herself in a cramped, untidy galley which smelled strongly of stale cigarettes and the lingering scent of an incense burner. There was a small kitchen area with a stove and miniature fridge, but the space was dominated by the sleeping area. Covered in what had probably once been a brightly coloured patchwork blanket, it was piled high with cushions.

Jake came in behind her and sat down on the edge of the bed. From underneath a cushion, he pulled out a packet of cigarettes and a box of matches. Without offering Maggie one, he lit up, narrowing his eyes as he blew a stream of smoke at her. Waving the cigarette vaguely at her he said, 'Strip.'

Maggie gaped at him as he made himself more comfortable on the cushions, preparing to watch her.

'What are you waiting for?' he asked when she did not immediately comply.

His voice was hard, but there was a resonance to his tone which betrayed his excitement. If she hadn't recognised it, Maggie knew she would probably have left at once. As it was she responded to his almost misogynistic disregard for her feelings, knowing she would enjoy his eventual capitulation to her all the more for it.

Holding his eye, she began to unfasten the buttons of her blouse. Her hair fell forward in a soft, dark curtain as she looked down. She shivered at the first touch of the air against her bare skin as she pulled the blouse from her waistband.

After that first, perfunctory slaking of their lust, Maggie sensed that there was time to savour this second encounter. Throwing off her blouse, she smiled to herself as Jake's eyes widened at the sudden exposure of her bare breasts. If she was expecting compliments she was doomed to disappointment, for the silence hung heavily between them as Maggie rolled her skirt down over her hips, closely followed by her sodden panties.

'Leave the shoes,' he instructed when she bent to take them off, 'but stay like that, with your tits hanging down and your arse in the air.'

The crudeness of his words made Maggie shudder and she closed her eyes momentarily so that he would not see the effect he was having on her. But he had seen and he chuckled softly as he moved forward to cup her breasts.

'Is this where you want it this time?' he asked her,

pressing them together to form a deep, shadowed valley.

Maggie sighed raggedly, imagining his cock sliding between them, his hot, thick sperm spattering her skin. Jake was watching her, his head slightly on one side as if trying to decide how he wanted her.

'Up on the bed,' he said suddenly, patting a spot beside him.

Maggie knelt awkwardly on the bed, her high heels spiking dangerously behind her.

'Yeah, that's it. Face away from me – arse high. Lean on your elbows. I want to look at you.'

He did not touch her and Maggie began to tremble as she imagined his gaze probing the most intimate parts of her. Her skin seemed to tingle with awareness, her sex becoming wetter and more swollen with every second that he scrutinised her. She could feel his breath whisper across her skin and knew that he was very close. She closed her eyes as she heard him stub out his cigarette.

'Nice,' he said, his voice thickening. 'Spread your knees wider – show me everything.'

Maggie did as she was asked and almost came as she imagined how she looked in the girlie-mag pose he had engineered. Her sex must be gaping, advertising clearly the extent of her arousal, leaving him in no doubt how much she wanted him again.

She gasped as he touched her, his fingertips finding the burgeoning nub of her clitoris with unerring accuracy.

'Oh, please . . .' she whispered, moving her hips frantically when he kept his fingerpad motionless against the bud.

'That's it,' he whispered, his lips brushing her ear, 'frig yourself against me. Make yourself come.'

114

Maggie moaned, half in protest, half in agreement as her body began to rock of its own accord. The cleft of her bottom rubbed against his bare forearm as he pressed his fingers against her, but made her do all the work.

'Christ, you're hot,' he whispered against her hair.

His tongue traced the whorls of her ear as she began to move faster, waggling her bottom as she neared crisis point. Her mouth fell open and she began to pant, past caring how she looked or what he might think of her, she wanted only to reach that peak which was fast coming into sight. Then, just as she felt she would vault into the abyss, Jake withdrew his hand and denied her.

Maggie groaned loudly and collapsed on to her stomach. Rolling over she caught sight of Jake's superior smile and saw red.

'You bastard!' she shouted, lashing out at him.

He laughed, incensing her so that he had to grab her wrists and wrestle her into submission. At last she felt the full length of his body against hers. The feel of it, still fully clothed, only served to fuel Maggie's frustration and she undulated frantically underneath him, pressing her pelvis against his to feel the delicious hardness at his groin pressed against her.

'Bastard,' she whispered, with less conviction this time.

There was something devilish about his smile, but she took comfort from the fact that he was as aroused as she. Her body felt as though it was vibrating, held on the verge of fulfilment like a finely strung bow. Their eyes met and for a moment time seemed to stand still, the tension between them stretched so taut.

Jake seemed to take pity on her, for this time when

he reached for her, his fingers curled into the soft, wet folds of her flesh and moved in expert circles around her clitoris. Maggie clung to him, arching her back and throwing back her head as the electric sensations surged through her.

'Don't stop,' she pleaded breathlessly, 'please don't, I can't bear it.'

Pleasure almost bordered on the most exquisite pain as she teetered on the edge. Then Jake tapped his finger firmly against the quivering nub of her clitoris, once, twice, three times, and suddenly her orgasm burst through her like an explosion of light.

Maggie writhed on the bed, incoherent sounds of joy tumbling from her lips as it went on and on.

'Easy, easy now.'

Gradually she became aware that he was speaking softly to her, gentling her, his fingers stroking along the slippery channels of her sex and rimming the entrance to her body. Maggie opened her eyes and looked at him.

'Come inside me?' she whispered.

Jake shook his head. Giving her sex an almost affectionate squeeze, he smeared his sticky fingers across her mouth.

'I want you to suck me.'

Maggie drew his fingers into her mouth and circled them with her tongue. Jake's eyes darkened as he watched the movement of her lips and she felt a jolt of power so strong it intensified the aftershocks still running through the centre of her.

'I like a man who knows what he wants,' she murmured when he withdrew his fingers.

Jake said nothing, merely leaning back against the cushions and watching her. There was an insolence in his eyes that amused her, an arrogance in the way he waited for her to undress him that kept her on the verge of re-arousal. He obviously had expected her to merely unfasten his jeans, but Maggie was determined that she would have her way, if only in this, and see him totally naked.

He was silent as she pulled his T-shirt up over his head, merely lying back and watching her as she ran her eyes over the body she had revealed. To her surprise his chest was covered in a thick, curling mat of hair. It thinned as it reached his belly, arrowing downward and disappearing into the waistband of his jeans.

His stomach was flat, the muscles well defined, tensing as Maggie lay her hand across them. Moving her hands up, across his chest, she splayed her fingers across his pectorals, feeling the flat, masculine nipples harden against her skin. His chest hair was coarse, yet surprisingly soft. It felt springy under her fingers and she spent a few moments running her hands across it, enjoying the feel of it against her skin.

Sensing that he was growing impatient, Maggie turned her attention to the fastening of his jeans. The buttons slipped easily through the buttonholes, despite the tumescence which stretched the fabric. He raised his hips slightly to help her as she pulled the jeans down his legs, leaving him completely naked.

He had a fine body, the skin silky beneath its covering of hair, the muscles hard and well-toned. His penis lay flat against his belly, pointing up towards his navel. The whiteness of his cock-skin looked out of place against its tanned and dark-haired surrounds and Maggie could see the thick vein on its underside throbbing gently as he watched her.

Glancing at him from beneath her lashes, she saw the small pulse beating in his jaw and knew that she was winning; he was quickly losing the initiative. His need was now as great as hers had been earlier.

Hiding her smile behind her hair, Maggie lowered her head and licked a trail along the underside of his cock, from its base to the tender slit at its end. Jake's thighs quivered and she heard him catch his breath as she opened her lips and drew the tip of his penis into the hot, wet cavity of her mouth. She didn't move, just held him there, paying him back a little for the way he had made her work for her own climax before.

Jake leaned forward and exerted a gentle pressure against the nape of her neck. Maggie did not have the will to resist, she merely closed her eyes and allowed his cock to slip to the back of her throat before drawing her lips back along its length.

She had intended to tease him a little, to play with him, but Jake would not let her. She felt him swell in her mouth and she cupped his balls with her hand, feeling the heat and weight of them. His fingers tangled in her hair and urged her to suck harder, faster; clearly he had no patience with her leisurely approach. It didn't matter, Maggie was enjoying the taste and feel of him – if he wanted it fast and furious, she was more than happy to deliver.

The skin across his scrotum had tightened so that it was silky-smooth beneath her fingers and she could feel the throbbing begin along the length of his shaft. It would not be long before his seed would surge through him and spill into her eager mouth, and Maggie rejoiced in the knowledge that she was rapidly bringing him to the point of no return.

Once again, Jake denied her the upper hand, withdrawing suddenly from her mouth and flipping her over on to her stomach. Shoving several cushions unceremoniously beneath her belly, he raised her

118

bottom high and spread her thighs apart with his hands.

'I love your arse,' he said, his voice low and urgent. 'It opens for me like a spilt peach.'

As if to demonstrate, he parted her buttocks and stroked the sensitive skin of her crease. His finger lingered at the forbidden orifice of her anus and for a moment Maggie thought that he would enter her. Then she felt the hard tip of his penis pressing against the pulpy flesh of her sex and she braced herself for his entry.

To her surprise, he did not take her with the near savagery he had used before, rather he slipped gently inside her, twisting his hips slightly so that she felt as though she was being stroked on the inside by a dozen sensitive fingers. Arching his back, he held his upper body away from her, taking most of his weight on his knees and the lower part of his legs.

His hands splayed against her spread bottom-cheeks, his thumbs caressing the crease between them and probing at her anus. Maggie felt herself open up to him as one thumb breached the sphincter and pressed against the fleshy tube which separated digit and cock.

Something seemed to click in Maggie's head and she wriggled her bottom restlessly, desperate for a deeper penetration. This time he did not disappoint her, pressing his thumb into her anal passage up to the second knuckle and turning it whilst at the same time sinking deeper into her, until she felt the ticklish slap of his balls against her perineum.

Bringing his second hand up to support her lower belly, he pressed carefully upwards, so that the entire area was compressed and she was barely able to distinguish one sensation from the other. In the back of her mind, she heard Gina telling her that Jake Curran fucked like an angel. Now she knew what the other girl had meant – this man knew exactly what to do, when to do it, and just the right amount of pressure to exert.

Maggie felt full of him, rocking her bottom back and forth to meet his thrusts and deepen the penetration. After a few minutes, Jake upped the tempo, moving faster as he stimulated Maggie's clitoris with one thumb, in time with the other which was moving in and out of her anus. Deeper and deeper, until finally his cock knocked against the entrance to her womb, filling her with a rigid shaft of heated flesh.

Maggie grunted as her breasts scraped against the rough surface of the bed cover, their oversensitised tips sending delicious signals to the core of her pleasure, now being rolled between Jake's thumb and forefinger.

She came, at the same moment as he did, collapsing over her back with a whispered curse which was smothered by the harshness of his breathing. And as the tremors finally began to subside, Maggie was surprised to discover that her face was wet with tears.

They lay like that for several minutes, until, at last, Jake regained his breath and withdrew from her. He handed her tissues and watched as she pulled on her clothes. Gradually, Maggie realised that he hadn't once kissed her, or offered her a single tender word. It didn't matter, not really, but she found it odd. In her experience even the most impersonal encounter usually moved the participants to some degree of tenderness. Obviously, Jake marched to a different drum. He certainly didn't seem to be aware of any shortcomings during their encounter.

Once she was dressed, Maggie stood up. Jake lay

there, unselfconsciously naked, an unlit cigarette resting between his lips. He didn't say anything, and his expression was inscrutable, yet Maggie had the overwhelming feeling that he wanted her to leave.

'I'll see myself out then, shall I?' she said ironically when he still did not speak.

'If you like.'

Maggie stared at him in astonishment. Was he really not going to offer to run her back to the hotel on his bike? The walk along the cliff top was not a long one, but surely basic etiquette dictated that he should at least offer to take her.

'I'm not exactly dressed for walking,' she pointed out reasonably.

Jake's eyes ran lazily over her from top to toe. 'Do you want a lift?' he asked her, taking the cigarette out of his mouth.

Perversely, now he had offered, Maggie found she didn't want to accept. 'No – I'll enjoy the walk.'

He looked at her as if he couldn't understand what she was waiting for. 'Did you want something?' he asked her with an insolent lift of one eyebrow.

Anger suddenly got the better of Maggie. 'Aren't you even going to see me off the boat?' she demanded, placing her hands on her hips aggressively.

Jake merely looked amused. 'No.'

'Bastard!'

'Bitch,' he replied, without rancour.

Maggie shook her head in wonder. 'Right. I'm leaving now.'

Watching him, she expected more than the slight cock of his head on one side. 'Goodbye,' she said.

Not waiting for him to reply, Maggie simply turned away and left him. Once off the boat, she turned

towards the cliff path. She'd been walking for some
moments before it occurred to her that, not only had
he never kissed her, but he hadn't mentioned seeing
her again either. To her surprise, she realised that i
mattered to her. It mattered to her very much.

Chapter Eight

O ver the next few days, Maggie was irritated to find that she was unable to concentrate on even the simplest task. Her mind kept sliding back to the time she had spent with Jake, her body stirring at the recollection as she relived every moment. Somehow the fact that Jake was not connected with the hotel imbued him with an aura of excitement, a sense almost of the elicit, and Maggie's preoccupation fed on itself, so that in the end the encounter was blown out of all proportion.

Lena, back at work after a few days rest, noticed her distraction and questioned her endlessly about it.

'For heaven's sake, Lena, let it rest, won't you?' Maggie snapped at her after the girl asked her what was wrong for the third time in an hour.

Lena didn't reply and Maggie forced herself not to look up from the spreadsheet she was studying . The other girl's hurt at her tone was palpable and Maggie instantly felt guilty. At last, she sighed and raised her eyes. Across the desk from her, Lena was weeping soundlessly, and Maggie felt a pang of remorse.

'Oh, Lena, please don't cry. You mustn't take any notice of me, I – '

'It's my fault, isn't it? I've done something wrong.'

Appalled, Maggie stood and, walking round the desk, went to put her arms around the girl. Lena turned her face away, but allowed Maggie to stroke her hair.

'Whatever makes you think that you're to blame?' Maggie asked gently.

'Isn't it true, then?' Lena said, her voice small, her head turning a fraction towards Maggie hopefully.

'Of course not.'

Lena, still sitting, turned her face towards Maggie, pressing it into the warm valley between her breasts. Maggie continued to stroke her hair, conscious of the warmth of Lena's breath through the thin silk of her blouse. After a few moments, Lena's lips moved against the soft curve of the underside of her breast, sending a small thrill through Maggie's body. Lena's mouth was hot against the slippery fabric as she kissed the pliant flesh, flicking her tongue towards the burgeoning crest.

In the back of Maggie's mind, she worried that she should put a stop to this now – Lena was already far more dependent on her than was comfortable. But little shocks of pleasure were trickling down her spine and radiating out through the softer tissues of her body. Thinking about Jake meant she was in a constant state of heightened sexual tension and Lena was offering her a release, a way to assuage the need which was filling her every waking moment.

Dipping her head, she kissed the top of Lena's hair. Lena paused in her loving exploration of Maggie's breast and looked up at her, her eyes clear and trusting. Maggie read the adoration there and hesitated. She didn't want to be adored, to be held responsible. Then, unexpectedly, Lena grinned.

'Don't look so solemn.' Reaching up, she touched one finger against the corner of Maggie's mouth. Without taking her eyes from her soft lower lip, she said, her voice low and husky, 'I want you.'

Slowly, Maggie bent her knees so that she was crouching at eye level with Lena. She scanned her face, looking for signs of uncertainty, or desperation, but the other girl merely stared guilelessly back at her and all that Maggie could read in her eyes was lust. To hell with it – Lena was a grown-up, she knew what she was doing. All this soul searching and taking of responsibility was getting in the way of the pursuit of pleasure.

Smiling, Maggie moved her face so that it was inches away from Lena's. This close, the other woman's face took on a blurred edge and her eyes glistened, sparkling alluringly. Staring into Maggie's eyes, her lips parted and the tip of her tongue ran along the edge of her upper lip, moistening it. Both women held their breath as, almost imperceptibly, they swayed towards each other.

Their mouths touched, lightly, and Maggie moved her head slightly from side to side, stimulating the sensitive flesh with the lightest of butterfly caresses. She could feel Lena trembling and the tension flowing from her affected Maggie, making her stomach muscles clench and her breasts swell and harden beneath the flimsy fabric.

Slowly, Maggie reached out a hand and splayed it across Lena's small breast. It quivered slightly beneath the soft cotton of her top, the nipple harden-

125

ing and straining against the centre of Maggie's palm
Maggie began to caress her, massaging the firm flesh
in a slow, circular motion. Lena sighed raggedly, her
sweet breath brushing across Maggie's face

Parting her lips over Lena's, Maggie kissed her
pressing against her breast and with the other hand
she cupped Lena's cheek. The other girl's mouth
tasted of cherries as Maggie explored it with her
tongue. Lena's arms came about her and she slipped
her own arms around Lena, holding her close. Her
nipples rubbed against hers, the small friction setting
up a chain reaction from her breasts to her womb
Maggie felt her sex flesh swell and moisten, rubbing
against the cotton gusset of her panties as she shifted
position slightly.

Her legs beginning to cramp, Maggie sank forward
onto her knees still kissing the other girl. Her fingers
found the warm, soft flesh at the top of Lena's thigh
and rested there, enjoying the feel of the texture of
her skin against her fingertips. She was close enough
to the apex of her thighs to feel the heat of her sex, yet
Maggie held back, savouring the anticipation.

She smiled as she felt Lena reach down and mirrored her caress on her own thigh. Now there was the
double excitement of waiting to be touched as well as
waiting to touch, and Maggie felt a fresh rush of
moisture coat her labia as she spun out the moment
until both women were desperate for release.

Maggie moved first. Sliding her fingers slowly
against the silky skin of Lena's inner thigh, she raised
her eyebrows as she discovered that Lena was not
wearing any underwear. Her fingertips encountered
the soft, silky hair of her mons and tangled in the
damp curls which fringed her labia.

As she had expected, Lena's flesh was slick with

the thick dew of arousal and Maggie's fingers moved easily along the slippery folds of flesh until she penetrated her with two fingers. Lena caught her breath and her head fell back, her eyes closing as she shifted her bottom on the chair, granting Maggie easier access.

Moving gently inside her, Maggie explored the dark channel, relishing the play of Lena's muscles against her fingers. Slowly, she withdrew her fingers and ran them up, to the apex of her labia, where her clitoris had already slipped from its hood. It quivered at the first touch of her fingers against it, and Maggie stroked it lightly, moving her fingers round and round the stem until it swelled and hardened.

Lena's own fingers were feverish as she copied the movement against Maggie's sex, through the thin cotton of her panties. Impatient, Maggie broke away for long enough to slip them off, kicking them under the desk before sinking on to her haunches again. Immediately, Lena's fingers found the soft, pulpy flesh and traced the silky channels. Maggie moaned and resumed her rhythmic circling of Lena's now throbbing clitoris.

Fastening her lips on Lena's, Maggie rocked forward on her toes, forcing Lena's fingers deeper into her body and grinding her own pulsing bud against the other girl's wrist. She came, gasping, her legs trembling as she leaned forward and rested her head on Lena's narrow shoulder. She pressed on the hot little button of flesh which now stood proud of Lena's softer labia and felt it vibrate as all the nerve endings quivered and Lena joined her at the peak.

They hung on to each other for several minutes, waiting to recover their energy. When at last they drew apart, Maggie looked at Lena and saw that there

127

was still a hint of arousal in the other girl's eyes. Languorously, Maggie swept her eyes across Lena's flushed features and smiled.

'What is it?' she asked her softly.

Lena smiled back, though her eyes remained serious. 'Can we go upstairs to your room?'

Maggie raised her eyebrows. 'We ought to get on with what we were doing,' she protested half-heartedly. 'Why?'

'I want you to do something for me,' Lena replied, entwining her fingers with Maggie's and bringing her hand to press it against the damp hair of her pubis. 'Would you?'

'It depends. What do you want me to do?'

Lena looked at her levelly, her eyes shining with a fervour that made Maggie's legs feel weak.

'I want you to shave me.'

As she spoke, Lena moved Maggie's hand back and forth over her pubic hair so that it tickled across the back of her hand. Maggie watched the progress of their entwined fingers and felt a stab of excitement. She shaved her own pubis every other day, but the thought of doing it to another woman was more exciting than she could imagine.

'But it's so beautiful, Lena, such a lovely colour. Are you sure?'

Recognising Maggie's excitement at the prospect, Lena smiled. Reaching out her free hand, she touched the hair on Maggie's head in a gesture of tenderness.

'I want to look like you. I want to find out what it feels like. Will you do it for me?'

Maggie's throat felt dry as she nodded. Wordlessly they rose and, after making the necessary adjustments to their clothing, they made their way out of the office and up the stairs hand in hand to Maggie's suite of ooms. Once there, Maggie drew the curtains and witched on the lamps on either side of the bed. She ound towels and spread one over the bedcover.

'Take off your skirt,' she said.

Maggie knew that her own eyes probably held the ame expression as Lena's – over-bright with unmiti-;ated excitement. Despite her recent climax her sex elt moist and heavy, her clitoris throbbing with a lull pulse as she watched Lena do as she was bid.)ressed only in a tight, blue jersey top and high heels he presented an alluring sight. On an impulse, ∕Iaggie went to the drawer of her dressing table and ook out her camera.

'Would you mind if I photographed you?' she sked.

Lena looked uncertain, her eyes flickering ner-ously from Maggie's face to the camera and back gain. 'Like this?'

'Before and after. And during. It might be interest-ng, don't you think?'

Lena seemed to come to a sudden decision. 'All ight. So long as it's for our eyes only.'

Maggie smiled. 'Of course.'

Loading up the camera with film, Maggie shot off a ew snaps of Lena standing in front of the bed.

'Lie down,' she said, nodding towards the towel he had spread across the duvet.

'On my back?'

Maggie nodded. Lena lay down and gazed up at ∕Iaggie through wide eyes as Maggie photographed er.

'Like this?'

'You could open your legs – keep them straight – hat's it. Good. A bit wider.'

Bending to take a closer shot, Maggie saw that Lena

was turned on by the act of being photographed
Every line of her lovely body displayed her tension
from the taut muscles in her thighs to the quivering
of her belly as Maggie brushed her fingers delicately
over the soft surface. Leaning over her, she swept her
lips across her forehead and down the side of her face.

'Bend your knees up,' she whispered.

Lena obeyed, but slowly, first one leg, then the
other. Maggie watched through half-closed eyes as
the lips of her sex peeled apart to reveal the rosy inner
labia and the dark, shadowed entrance to her body.
Moisture glistened at the lip of her vagina and clung
to the fine red hairs which grew along either side.

Maggie ran her fingertip lightly along first one
channel, then the other, wiping the residue away.
Then she finished the film in the camera, using Lena's
soft, white thighs to frame the picture of her sex in
the centre of the shot.

'You're so beautiful,' Maggie told her, 'I love looking at you.'

She ran her eyes over Lena's slender, lightly freckled legs and marvelled at the delicacy of the colour
of her skin. Only a true redhead could have that
almost alabaster-looking white skin, that delicious
smattering of freckles.

'Wait,' she said softly.

Changing the film in the camera, Maggie put
aside and went into the bathroom. She kept all her
shaving equipment in one large cabinet, apart from
her other toiletries. Shaving herself, keeping her
mound smooth and depilated, had become a ritual,
rite which she performed regularly with practised
care.

Taking out the large glass bowl, she half filled
with warm water. Then she selected a fresh razor and

130

put it and the soap and oil on a tray together with a small towel and a pair of scissors. It had been Antony who had shaved her the first time. Just thinking about that first experience made Maggie feel weak with remembered lust.

He had been so careful, so exact, and she remembered with a vividness that still made her shudder how vulnerable she had felt as he had denuded her, how open and helpless. It had been a significant act of trust to allow him to perform so intimate a service, yet she had surrendered herself to his ministrations gladly. Now she was about to enable Lena to experience the same feeling as she had all those months ago, and she felt privileged.

Lena hadn't moved from the position in which Maggie had left her, but her eyes opened wide as she saw what she was carrying. Laying the tray on the bedside table, Maggie raised her eyebrows at her.

'What's wrong? Are you having second thoughts?'

Lena shook her head, but she continued to eye the tray warily. 'No, I – I suppose I was expecting an electric razor. Silly really.'

Maggie laughed softly. 'Oh no. There's nothing like a wet shave – ask any man. There's an art to this, Lena, and a commitment. Pay attention now; you'll have to learn to do this yourself.'

To that end, Maggie brought a small, round shaving mirror from the bathroom and positioned it between Lena's legs so that she could see herself. Fetching more cushions, she pushed them under Lena's head to give her a clear view.

'Now, it's important that you should relax.'

It was obvious from the way she held herself taut that Lena was not going to be able to do that. She

131

flinched at the first touch of cold metal against her mons and Maggie paused, scissors poised.

'Trust me,' she said softly.

Lena held her eye for a moment, then she nodded. 'I trust you, Maggie,' she whispered.

'Relax, then. Lie back on the pillows.'

Lena did as she was asked, but her eyes slid to the mirror propped between her ankles and stayed there as Maggie began to trim the hair which grew between her legs.

Maggie cut it so that only half an inch remained all over her mound. Already the pale-pink skin was visible beneath the light furring of hair and Maggie paused to record it on camera. Lena appeared fascinated, stroking her palm in the direction that the hair grew as if it were not a part of her, but something new and unfamiliar.

'Do you want me to go on?' Maggie asked, watching her.

Lena caught her eye and nodded. Holding her gaze, Maggie gently pushed her knees further apart, exposing her more fully. She smiled as Lena caught her lower lip between her teeth, then she turned her attention to trimming the wispy hairs which fringed the delicate folds of her labia.

It was difficult to ignore the clear evidence of Lena's arousal, for Maggie knew she was in the same state. But she could not afford to have anything other than a steady hand and she forced herself to concentrate on the rhythmic snip of the scissors at the crinkly hair.

When, at last, she was satisfied, Maggie squeezed a generous portion of shaving cream into the palm of her hand and began to massage it into the remaining hair. Lena was breathing heavily now, her small breasts rising and falling rapidly under the soft jersey top. Careful not to touch the sensitive vulval flesh, Maggie worked up a lather before wiping her hands on the small towel and picking up the razor.

The atmosphere of sex in the room was by now so thick that Maggie could not help but be affected by it. Yet her hand was sure as she made the first track through the white cream with the razor. The sound of the metal chinking against the glass bowl, the swish of the razor head in the water, Lena's sudden intake of breath – all these sounds seemed magnified by the tension of the moment.

Soon the mound of Lena's pubis was smooth and hairless. Inspecting her handiwork minutely, Maggie rinsed away the residue of shaving cream and patted it dry carefully with the small towel. It was the outer labia which would be tricky and she could sense Lena was literally holding her breath as she ran the razor along the vulnerable flesh.

She looked up and smiled as she swirled it in the now milky water and returned to attend to the other side.

'Almost there,' she said conversationally, though her stomach was churning with barely suppressed desire.

The reality of having the other woman lying, open, completely at her mercy was having a profound effect on her. She wanted to kiss the freshly exposed skin, to lick and suck at the vulnerable flesh until Lena was crying out for her to stop.

'Open wider,' she said, aware that her voice had grown throaty.

With her fingertips, she applied more cream to the exposed skin of Lena's inner buttocks. This was where Maggie had been tattooed and she knew how sensitive an area it could be. Lena shivered as she removed the last of her pubic hair and rinsed and dried her skin. Shorn, her sex looked exposed and vulnerable, the skin slightly reddened from its contact with the razor.

'It looks so – so odd,' Lena sounded disappointed and Maggie smiled reassuringly at her.

'You'll get used to it,' she said, picking up the bottle of oil and applying it liberally to the depilated skin. 'I think it's beautiful.'

'Do you?' Lena asked her hopefully.

Maggie merely smiled, concentrating on working the oil into the tender skin. Gradually, her fingers slipped lower, encountering the heavier, warmer juices which coated the channels of the other girl's sex. Lena moaned and relaxed back against the pillows. Maggie could feel the tension flowing out of her as she sought and found the hard little nub which was at the centre of her arousal.

She could smell the sweet musk of her feminine secretions and that, mingled with the perfume of the oil, played on her senses, making her head swim. Lena's denuded mound was shining, slippery with oil, and her labia were flushed a deep, rosy pink.

Giving in at last to temptation, Maggie dipped her head and, holding her open with the fingers of one hand, she kissed her sex as she would her mouth, swirling her tongue around her entrance. Lena's fingers meshed in her hair as Maggie eased the tip of her tongue inside her and moved it in and out.

'Oh yes! Maggie, oh God that's so good. Yes. Fuck me with your tongue. Deeper, much deeper, ohh!'

Maggie felt Lena's clitoris pulse against her lips as the first waves of orgasm broke and she brought her tongue up to flick at the throbbing bud until Lena cried out for her to stop.

Lifting her head, Maggie smiled and climbed onto the bed. Pushing Lena's legs still wider apart, she straddled her so that her own open sex lips covered hers. Their juices mingled as Maggie rocked back and forth, stimulating herself against Lena's sated flesh. Closing her eyes, she imagined herself filled by Jake and she ground down harder, butting her clitoris against the other girl's until she came, the sensations surging through her like a torrent.

'Oh Jake,' she groaned, pressing the heel of her hand against her pulsing sex and rolling away from Lena. Easing three fingers inside her body, she moved them slowly in and out as the last tremors swept through her.

It was only gradually that she became aware of Lena's appalled silence. Opening her eyes, she saw the other girl's anguished expression and at once she realised her mistake.

'Lena, I – '

'Who's Jake?' Lena said, flinching away when Maggie reached for her.

Maggie groaned inwardly, cursing herself for her lack of control. 'A man I'm seeing – '

'Seeing?' Lena interrupted her again. 'You mean you're sleeping with him at the same time as you're sleeping with me?'

'Well – '

'When was the last time?' she demanded, sitting up in the bed and glaring at Maggie with indignation.

Maggie rolled off the bed and dressed calmly, while all the time her mind was racing. She felt cornered by Lena's questions, and she resented the feeling. Lena had no right to make her feel trapped like this.

'This isn't an exclusive relationship, Lena, you know that.'

'But you love me.'

It was a statement, not a question and Maggie felt exasperated. 'Don't start that again, Lena. We've just enjoyed great sex together – don't spoil it.'

Lena looked horrified. 'Is that all it is to you? Just sex?'

Maggie gazed at Lena and felt her stomach plummet. This was too much. She felt irritated, exasperated and remorseful all at once.

'Don't do this, Lena,' she warned.

Lena chose to ignore the warning. 'I love you. If you'd just give us a chance, stay faithful for a while, you'd feel the same way, you'd see – '

'No I wouldn't,' Maggie interrupted firmly. Sighing, she ran a hand through her hair. 'Look, Lena, I don't want to hurt you. If you can't enjoy this relationship for what it is, then we must end it, right now.'

'No.'

'Yes. Don't you see? All this, it's tedious. The sex isn't worth it. I'm sorry if that sounds harsh, but that's the way it is.'

Lena began to cry, but this time her tears moved Maggie to anger rather than pity. 'Oh for heaven's sake, grow up. We've had fun, but now it's time to get dressed and go back to work.'

Lena stopped crying instantly. 'But I love you,' she said pathetically.

'You'll soon find someone else to take my place.'

'No I won't. Never.'

Maggie glanced at her and was disconcerted by the directness of her gaze. It was implacable and she felt a shiver of apprehension travel up her spine. Suddenly she felt claustrophobic: whereas before she had wanted her, now all she wanted was to get as far away from Lena as possible.

'You'll have to,' she said firmly. 'I'm going out for a short while – field any problems, please, until I get back.' Before Lena had a chance to say any more, Maggie had slipped into her shoes and was out of the bedroom.

It was a relief to get out into the fresh air. The confrontation with Lena had shaken her, especially as it had come out of the blue. Heading towards the cliff path, Maggie decided she had been right to break it off. That was what she should have done before, she could see that now. There was no room in her life for a possessive partner, male or female.

Maggie felt a pang of regret – she genuinely liked Lena and their friendship could have been mutually satisfying. She hoped that Lena wouldn't be too upset for long, but it really was a case of having to be cruel to be kind. After all, she had no desire to become the kind of person Lena wanted her to become, and it was better in the long run to be honest.

The day was hot and sultry, the sea stretching to her right was a deep, crystal tipped blue. As she drew closer to the estuary Maggie was conscious that her step had quickened and she had to make a deliberate effort not to break into a run.

Since her encounter with Jake she had forced herself not to walk to the estuary, determined that he should be the one to make the next move. The fact that he had made no attempt whatsoever to contact her had both angered and excited her. She wasn't used to men playing hard to get.

She could have questioned Gina about his where-abouts, of course, but she had her pride and, besides, she would rather the whole hotel did not know about any life she might have outside its four walls. But now that she found herself heading towards his houseboat, Maggie had a strong urge to see him, if only to say hello. It might be ridiculous, but she felt like a young girl on her way to a date.

Maggie laughed aloud at the irony of that. Jake was hardly her idea of a dream date, not by any stretch of the imagination. It was a novel feeling nevertheless and she was almost running as she approached the brow of the hill from which she would be able to see his boat.

Her disappointment when she realised it wasn't moored in its usual spot hit her like a blow to the solar plexus. Her mouth hung open as the air left her in a small exclamation of distress. He'd left. He'd actually gone away without so much as a nod of farewell in her direction.

Maggie stared for several minutes at the spot where his boat had been moored. Aware that the feeling was irrational – what claim could she possibly think she had on him anyway? She recognised the emotion churning through her as rejection. Was this how Lena had felt when she had spurned her?

Impatient with the thought – this was quite different, after all – Maggie turned back the way she had come. Slowly as she re-trod the path, disappointment solidified into indignation. To hell with Jake if he had forgotten the thrill of their coming together so soon. No doubt she had built it up in her mind anyway. It was only the novelty of not being in control that had made it seem so exciting to her.

After all, at the hotel she could have anyone, man or woman, she didn't need the likes of Jake Curran. Yes – to hell with him, she didn't need him at all.

Chapter Nine

George was standing at the door of the hotel. Something about his stance warned Maggie that he was looking for her and she quickened her pace. One look at his face told Maggie that there was a problem and her stomach turned over as she broke into run.

'What is it? What's happened?'

'Another fire – in the garden this time.'

'Oh no!'

Maggie groaned and followed George round the side of the hotel to the tennis courts. She could smell the smoke now and her heart hammered in her chest as she worried about what she would find. The fire service were already there, tackling the blaze which, Maggie saw now, was devouring the shed where all the tennis equipment was kept.

Brett Tunnock was at the forefront, directing his men as they brought the flames under control. Seeing Maggie, he shouted an order, then strode over to meet her. His expression was stern, his face grimy as he passed his sleeve over his forehead and took off his helmet. Maggie noticed that he looked tired; the skin around his eyes was crinkled through lack of sleep and, for once, he looked his age.

'This is getting to be a habit,' he said without preamble.

'Is it arson again?' Maggie was dismayed, though a small part of her was glad that, this time, there was no doubt that Jake Curran was not involved. He might be a bastard, but at least he wasn't trying to put her out of business.

'Looks like it.' Brett glanced over to the shed and shouted at one of his men who had gone in too close. 'I have to go – be available to speak to me once we're done here, all right?'

'Of course.'

Maggie frowned, watching him stride away from her. She worried at her lower lip with her teeth. Having an arsonist in their midst was hardly going be good for business. Her mind working on the problem of containing the damage to their public image, Maggie turned away and went inside.

Above her, Lena watched the proceedings from the safety of her bedroom. The flames danced and twisted, defying the best efforts of the fire fighters to bring them under control. She hugged herself tightly, unable to contain her glee. Her breasts hardened as she watched and she pressed her palms over the burgeoning crests, caressing herself lazily as she watched the fire leap and flicker.

She felt warm, languorous even, as if she was lying naked in front of the fire, her skin turning a rosy pink, toasting in the firelight. Lena shuddered, expelling her breath on a long sigh. Desire churned through her with an urgency that left her gasping. Pressing the heel of her hand against the gentle mound of her lower belly, she slid it downwards, pressing the fabric of her skirt between her legs and stimulating the somnolent flesh of her vulva.

Impatient now, Lena rucked up her skirt and slipped her fingers inside her briefs. Her shaven mons felt soft and unfamiliar, the moist channels of her sex less so. Feverishly, she ran her fingers back and forth, settling on the apex of her labia where her clitoris throbbed and pulsed with life.

As if through a curtain of gauze, Lena watched the men outside fight to subdue the fire she had created. She felt at one with the elements, exultant that she could wreak such havoc, so easily. Bearing down, she rubbed at her sensitive flesh, bringing herself to orgasm quickly. Leaning her forehead against the cool glass of the window, she closed her eyes as the shards of sensation sliced through her. Below the fire still fizzed and spat in defiance.

It would have been even better if it had been dark. Lena frowned, annoyed with herself for not waiting. But the urge had been too compelling, the draw of the flames too strong to resist. Slowly, she withdrew her hand from her panties and smoothed down her skirt.

Maggie had seen the fire. Lena's face hardened. Maggie. She didn't know what she had tried to throw away. It was a good thing that she, Lena, did not give up so easily. Otherwise Maggie would never know the true depth of her love. A love that could set the world on fire. Lena smiled, feeling happy suddenly.

The fire was almost out now, the last of the flames flickering weakly, defeated. Then it was over. Nothing left but ashes.

* * *

Brett Tunnock strode into Maggie's office a few minutes later.

'This time there really will have to be an investigation,' he told her.

Maggie sighed. If word got out about this it might well close them down. 'I suppose you're right. Is it possible to be discreet? Most of my clients would turn tail and run if they thought that their presence here might become public.'

Brett regarded her thoughtfully. 'I've heard rumours about this place – is it true what they say?'

'What do they say?'

Brett fiddled with the brim of his helmet, his eyes fixed on Maggie's. 'Most of the locals reckon it's a regular den of iniquity.'

Maggie laughed. 'We're all consenting adults,' she said flippantly, aware that she hadn't answered his unspoken questions.

'You too?' he probed, his eyes following her every move as she walked over to the window.

Maggie stared out towards the Atlantic, her mind drifting out with the tide. 'Oh, especially me,' she said vaguely.

She sensed Brett move towards her, caught the distinctive scent of his skin, and was reminded of the day he had kissed her, here in this very room. If they hadn't been interrupted by his pager . . . 'Brett,' she murmured, turning towards him.

He was standing very close, but he made no attempt to take her into his arms. Maggie stared back at him, a quizzical expression in her eyes.

'Is there anyone who might have a grudge against this hotel, or you personally?'

'Pardon?' Maggie frowned, disorientated.

'Maybe you've fired someone, or have a disgruntled guest?'

At last his words penetrated the fog of sensuality which had enveloped her. So that was the way he had decided to play it – straight by the book. Maggie smiled mischievously.

'Absolutely not. None of our guests leaves here feeling disgruntled. Satisfaction is guaranteed at the Black Orchid.' Reaching out, she ran the tip of her forefinger provocatively down the front of his lapel. 'You ought to book in for a few days – I could design you a de-stress package. We'd send you out feeling on top of the world.'

Brett captured her hand and brought it up to his lips. They were warm and soft against the tender join between her forefinger and thumb.

'I'm sure you would,' he murmured. 'But I'm not sure I could sleep at night knowing you have a pyromaniac running amok on the premises.'

Maggie gave an exaggerated pout and leaned forward to kiss him lightly on the corner of his mouth. 'You really know how to turn a girl on,' she laughed softly. Moving away from him, she turned her mind to the problem in hand. 'I can't really believe that someone on my staff could be responsible,' she admitted after a few moments.

'Do you deal with all the hiring and firing?'

'Yes. My assistant, Lena, she helps, but I conduct all the interviews personally.' She smiled. 'I'm not aware of any dissatisfaction amongst the staff – the perks we offer here are second to none.'

To her amusement, Brett appeared flustered by her words. It was quite a novelty for her to encounter quite such a *straight* man, and Maggie knew that she would enjoy sleeping with him, when the time came.

And the time would come, of that she was sure. Meanwhile, she could simply relish the anticipation.

'Don't look so shocked, Brett – I believe in looking after my staff.'

'I just bet you do.'

He grinned at her suddenly and the strange tension that had enveloped them was dissipated. They both turned at the knock on the door.

'Come in,' Maggie said wearily.

It was Gina, the receptionist. She looked worried and Maggie's heart sank still further.

'I'm sorry to barge in, Maggie, but I thought you ought to know there's about to be a mass exodus of the clients. Already a good third have checked out and from the number of requests for help with packing and porterage, we'll soon be empty.'

Brett made a rueful face at Maggie and moved towards the door. 'I can see you're going to be busy, so I'll see myself out. I'll be in touch in a couple of days.'

Maggie nodded and waved, distracted by the ledger placed in front of her by Gina.

'What reasons are being given?'

'They seem to think that someone on the staff is bound to ring the *News of the World* to tell them that the hotel is being systematically burnt down, and the place will soon be swarming with press.'

'But that's ridiculous.'

'I know, but what can you say?' Gina shrugged.

'I suppose you can't blame them.' Maggie pointed at two names in the register. 'These two, for example – the press would have a field day if they were discovered in the same room together.'

'I shouldn't think their respective husbands would

144

be too chuffed either,' Gina giggled. 'What are we going to do?'

Maggie sat down with a sigh. 'Well, we can't do much to stop those who want to go. The problem is that everyone else will follow like lemmings. Let's hope we can get the inquiry over with this week while we're quiet. How are our bookings for next week?'

Gina turned the page of the register and studied the entries, all made in Lena's neat hand.

'There's the Ladies' Club dinner on Tuesday – I've booked a drag act and arranged some discreet escorts just in case anyone wants to take things further. Then we've got a hen party on the Friday, so we're fully booked over the weekend. Apart from that, about half the rooms will be taken by individual guests from this Sunday onwards.'

Maggie passed a hand wearily over her eyes. Business was not looking good. 'Okay Gina – keep up the good work for me, will you? You're doing a great job.'

The girl's face lit up at the praise. 'Thanks Maggie. Oh, by the way,' she said as she reached the door, 'there was a phone call for you earlier.'

'Oh?'

'Yes. It was Jake Curran.'

Gina paused to study Maggie's reaction. Maggie, who had been unable to hide her quick flare of excitement, quickly brought her expression under control.

'Why on earth did he phone me?' she asked with what she hoped was appropriate sang-froid. One look at Gina's face told her that the other girl was not fooled.

'He said to tell you he'll be in the Fisherman's Pride at eight o'clock tonight.'

Maggie stared at Gina who was now regarding her with open curiosity.

'When – when did he call?'

'About an hour ago. You were dealing with the fire and I haven't had a chance to tell you until now.'

'Of course. Um – did he say anything else?'

'No. Just that he'd be there at eight. Maggie?'

'Yes?'

Gina looked troubled and Maggie gained the distinct impression that she was trying to decide whether or not to speak out. Embarrassed anyway that the girl had found out about her and Jake, Maggie was, for once, lost for words.

'Nothing,' Gina said after a moment. 'I'll get you a cup of coffee shall I? You look totally pooped.'

Maggie flashed her a grateful smile. 'Would you? Thanks.' Maggie turned away, relieved that Gina had decided not to comment on her liaison with Jake.

Why on earth had he telephoned? Sitting back in her swivel chair, Maggie allowed her mind to drift towards her errant lover. It was cruel of him to ask to speak to her through Gina, given that the two of them clearly had a longstanding on-off affair, but Gina hadn't seemed particularly worried about that. Did he expect Maggie to defer any plans she might have had for the evening to meet him at the pub he mentioned? She laughed aloud at the sheer audacity of the man. Who the hell did he think he was dealing with? Yet another of the love-struck females who, according to Gina, had littered his path since puberty.

'You sound happy.'

Maggie looked up in surprise as Lena came into the room. Eyeing her warily, she gave her a guarded smile.

'Hello Lena. Did you see the fire?'

A strange expression flitted across Lena's face, only for an instant, but Maggie noticed it and felt a moment's disquiet. The girl didn't seem in the least bit concerned about recent events and her reaction struck Maggie as being odd.

'Yes,' she said, moving over to the window where Maggie could no longer see her face, 'I saw it. Is Gina making your coffee?'

'She offered, yes,' Maggie replied guardedly. Lena had been upset when she left her earlier – that was probably why she seemed to be acting strangely now. What other reason could there possibly be?

Lena turned to her and asked quietly, 'Do you want me to resign?'

The light was behind her, so Maggie wasn't able to read her expression, but there was something about the levelness of her tone that told her Lena was perfectly serious.

'Why on earth would I want you to resign?' Maggie asked her, genuinely taken aback. She had not expected this.

'You might not want to run the risk of any awkwardness. I wouldn't want to be an embarrassment to you.'

Maggie sighed, running her hands wearily through her hair. So that was why Lena seemed odd – she was worried that the brief relationship between them and her reaction to its demise might jeopardise her job. Then another thought occurred to Maggie – maybe Lena *wanted* to leave, perhaps she thought that staying as they were would be more than she could take. The thought of losing her right-hand woman at such a difficult time made Maggie feel quite panicky.

'Oh Lena. I don't want you to leave, especially not at the moment. There's to be an inquiry into this latest

147

fire, half the guests have checked out, the press are likely to descend at any minute – would it help if I said "*please* stay"?' Glancing at Lena, she made a face. 'I need you.'

Lena's smile struck Maggie as being almost secretive, but she was relieved when the girl nodded.

'Of course I'll stay. I know you need me, Maggie – and I wouldn't abandon you now.'

Gina arrived then with the coffee. 'Oh!' she exclaimed when she saw Lena, 'I didn't realise you were here.'

'Obviously,' Lena remarked drily.

Would you like a cup?'

'Yes – if it isn't too much trouble.'

Maggie watched the two women with a sense of rising exasperation. It was as if they were vying with each other to do things for her, which was all very flattering, but she could do without the aggravation it caused. Did all her relationships at the hotel have to be so damn complicated?

She had to admit, that was one of the things that attracted her to Jake. There was nothing complicated, or difficult about their relationship. Each knew what the other wanted – sex, pure and simple. On an impulse she decided that she would meet him this evening, albeit on his terms. That settled, she set about the work that needed to be done with a lighter heart.

She saw him the moment she walked into the public bar of the Fisherman's Pride, which was half full, mostly with groups of men and the odd solitary drinker. Jake stood out in the crowd. There was a presence about him, an aura that marked him out as a loner. Someone to be avoided, not to be spoken to unless invited. Maggie felt her stomach clench and unclench with excitement.

The room fell silent as Maggie entered, all eyes swivelling towards her. She felt horribly conspicuous in her tight, red lycra minidress and she consciously squared her shoulders as she walked across to the bar and pulled out a high stool.

Jake turned and acknowledged her with his eyes, though he did not smile. He was leaning on the bar, a pint mug in front of him, his long hair loose about his shoulders. Tonight he was wearing a navy-blue T-shirt with a denim shirt worn open over it. His jeans were tight and well worn, his boots scuffed and, she noticed, in dire need of re-heeling.

'You came then.'

Taking her time, Maggie attracted the attention of the barman and ordered herself a dry Martini.

'Looks like it,' she replied at last, slipping up onto the stool. Aware that her dress had ridden up her thighs, she went to pull it down.

'Leave it.'

Maggie looked at Jake, indignation warring with desire. It was an unequal battle. Conscious of the glances she was attracting, she sipped her drink and waited for Jake to make the next move. Just sitting next to him gave her a thrill. For no reason she could cite, Maggie could feel the desire churning through her, as if every nerve ending was tuned to respond to his proximity.

'Where have you been?' she asked when she could bear the silence no longer.

Jake turned to her, his eyes mocking. 'Did you miss me?'

Maggie stared at him, unblinking, unsmiling, and she saw his pupils darken and dilate. He wasn't nearly as unaffected by her as his stance suggested, and that knowledge gave Maggie confidence.

'Where can we go?' she asked him, her voice low and urgent.

Jake's lips curved slightly. 'You really are a hot little bitch, aren't you?'

Maggie met his gaze steadily, her heart beating erratically in her chest. It didn't matter that everyone in the pub, it seemed, was staring at her, or that it would be obvious to anyone who cared to look that she wanted Jake. She knew that the puckered areolae of her nipples would be clearly evident through her dress, and that her bare legs were exposed almost to her groin. She didn't care. It only mattered that Jake should take her out of here and make love to her – now.

Slowly, so that only he could see, Maggie shifted slightly on the stool so that her legs moved apart, advertising the fact that she wasn't wearing anything underneath. Jake's eyes slid down to her crotch and a pulse twitched in his jaw. Maggie imagined the glimpse he had seen of her shaven mons, the swollen labia protruding wantonly between the exposed outer lips of her sex and she shivered.

Jake jerked his head towards a door on the other side of the room. Silently, Maggie put down her drink and slid off the stool. Ignoring the eyes that followed her, she walked to the door and waited for Jake to open it for her.

Inside, all was gloomy until Jake clicked on the light switch. A single pendant lamp lit up, illuminating the snooker table which almost filled the room. Closing the door behind him, Jake lodged a chair underneath the handle before turning to Maggie. His face was in shadow, but she could gauge his arousal by the way he held himself – taut, like a panther about to strike.

'Lift up your dress,' he sand, his voice low and resonant with desire.

Maggie lifted the hemline of her dress and slowly rolled it up, over her hips. She felt vulnerable, horribly exposed as she stood naked from the waist down, teetering slightly in her spindly, high-heeled sandals. She was trembling by the time Jake moved towards her.

His fingers splayed against the softly rounded flesh of her stomach, edging down to her vulva as he bent his head and kissed the curve of her neck. Swallowing hard, Maggie closed her eyes, her fingers reaching for the reassurance of his shirt beneath them.

'Christ, you're wet. You're like a bitch on heat.'

His whisper seemed loud in the claustrophobic little room, his breath tickling along the soft skin of her neck, making her shiver anew. Maggie's hand sought and found the betraying bulge at his groin and she squeezed gently, needing no words to point out that he was in the same state.

Suddenly Jake's icy control seemed to snap. Moving away from her he began to unbutton his fly. Maggie watched as his cock sprang from the opening, rock-hard and glistening, and her vulva fluttered in response to the visual stimulus.

Jake moved forward and, before she realised his intention, he picked Maggie up around the waist and sat her on the edge of the snooker table. It felt reassuringly solid beneath her, legs dangling over the edge, the cold wooden rim hard against her naked buttocks. Jake pushed her knees apart and stood between her thighs, the fabric of his jeans harsh against the soft flesh of her inner thighs. Maggie felt her sex lips part, opening in anticipation of the thrust of his hot penis into the depths of her body, and her breath caught in her chest.

Unexpectedly, Jake pushed his fingers through her hair, lifting it up and fanning it out around her face. Then slowly, he lowered her so that she was lying on her back on the green baize, the overhead light shining in her eyes. Jake knocked it as he leaned over her and it swung crazily back and forth as he held himself, poised, at the entrance to her body. Maggie watched the shadows play over his face, giving a dark, almost satanic cast to his features that made her pulse accelerate.

He circled her wrists and lifted her arms up above her head where he held them together easily with one hand. With the other hand he moulded one of her breasts beneath the soft, revealing lycra, kneading the tender flesh and passing his thumb back and forth across the aching nipple.

Maggie bit her lip, feeling helpless as he pinned her down on the table. She could feel her feminine secretions trickling slowly down between her buttocks, seeping on to the green baize. She felt hot, consumed by the combined heat of their bodies and she thrust her pelvis against his impatiently. The velvety head of his penis rubbed tantalisingly across the stretched membranes of her vulva, smearing her juices along the slippery channels of her sex.

'Please . . .' she whispered, barely aware that she'd spoken.

Jake leaned over her, his lips inches away from hers, his eyes glittering as he held her gaze. Letting go of her wrists, he placed his hands palms down on the table at either side of her waist. Then slowly, never taking his eyes from hers, he slipped inside her.

Maggie gasped, clenching her muscles so that she drew him in deeper. She whimpered, deep in her throat as he withdrew, bringing her arms up around his shoulders and holding onto him, urging him to thrust again, deeper. He did not disappoint her, burying the length of his shaft into the hot, slippery channel of her sex, filling her.

Bending her knees up, Maggie wrapped her legs around his waist. Jake groaned as he felt the pressure of the side of her stiletto heels dig into the taut flesh of his buttocks. Maggie pressed harder, urging him on. Her fingers meshed in his hair and she forced his head up, so that she could watch his face.

A fine film of sweat had broken out on his skin and it shone in the bright light. His eyes were dark and opaque, his expression glazed as he moved in and out of her with increasing tempo. *Now who has the upper hand?* Maggie thought silently, twisting her hips as his breath escaped him in a ragged sigh.

Shifting position slightly, she altered the angle of his entry so that his shaft, long and slippery now with her juices, rubbed against the epicentre of her pleasure. Eyes locked together in a silent battle of wills, they fucked silently, solemnly, each determined that the other should be the first to come.

Reaching down, between her thigh and his pelvis, Maggie cupped the hairy sacs of his balls and squeezed gently. The skin across his scrotum was stretched tight, the seed sacs inside full and hot. With perfect coordination Maggie milked them as she clenched her secret, innermost muscles, drawing the sperm from him in a sudden, uncontrollable spasm.

Jake cried out, his face contorting in a rictus of ecstasy as he pumped his seed into Maggie's triumphant body. The feel of his cock vibrating against the

153

silky, cleated walls of her vagina tipped Maggie over the edge and her internal muscles convulsed, squeezing the last of his emission from him and sending shockwaves of pleasure radiating through her body from her head to her toes.

Afterwards, Jake lay across her for a moment, catching his breath, his cock resting, quiescent, inside her body. It slipped out softly when he rose and he tucked it back into his jeans without saying a word. Silently, Maggie took a wad of tissues from her bag and cleaned herself. Then she stood up and rolled down her dress.

Jake was watching her, his eyes wary. Maggie smiled, feeling completely in control.

'That was very nice. Thank you,' she said coolly.

Turning on her heel she took the chair away from the door and opened it. She didn't look back at Jake as she left the room and, although aware of the curious eyes which followed her, she crossed the bar calmly and went outside to where she'd parked her car. Slipping into the driver's seat, she wound down the roof and inserted a CD.

She felt good. No, more than good, she felt terrific, elated. Having played Jake at his own game she knew that the next time they met it would be on a more equal footing. By the look on Jake's face as she had walked away, she knew that next time would not be long in coming.

Laughing to herself, Maggie fired the engine and drove away.

Chapter Ten

'*H*onestly, Antony, there's no point in your coming down. No, it's all right. You've got quite enough to do at the club as it is ...' Maggie lodged the telephone receiver under her chin and doodled on a notepad as Antony spoke. In truth, a part of her would have liked to have been able to say, yes, I do need a shoulder to lean on, but she knew that would not do her any good in the long run. She was known to be able to cope in a crisis, and, by God, cope she would!

'Maybe I'll come down and visit you – have myself pampered for a couple of days,' she suggested lightly.

'We could swap,' he countered, 'you run the club while I get the hotel back on track.'

Maggie bristled defensively. 'The hotel isn't *off* the track,' she told him indignantly. 'Really, Tony, it's nothing I can't handle.'

'You sound very calm, considering,' he commented shrewdly.

Maggie smiled and stretched. The phone had been

ringing when she walked through her office door after her meeting with Jake and she still felt keyed up.

'I've been having myself a good time,' she confided.

'Oh? With the delectable Lena, I presume?'

Maggie laughed. 'You're such an old gossip,' she teased. 'Actually my relationship with Lena has proved rather short lived. I'm looking in other directions right now.'

'Other directions? Oh God, Maggie – you don't mean that disreputable ruffian who lives on a houseboat?'

Maggie laughed at Antony's tongue-in-cheek description of Jake. 'How did you guess?'

'I know you Maggie. I told you, didn't I? I knew you were ripe for a bit of rough.'

'Antony, you're outrageous.'

'No, just perceptive. So – was he worth it?'

Maggie swivelled in her seat and gazed out into the darkness through her uncurtained window. 'Hmmm. I'm reserving final judgement though. He is a bit of a rogue.'

Antony's warm chuckle came over the line, caressing her across the miles. He sounded very close, almost as if he was speaking to her from the next room. 'You be careful. Play with fire and you could get your fingers burned.'

'Very funny, especially in the light of recent events.'

'You know what I mean, Maggie. I know this guy has caught your interest, but don't forget, he doesn't play by our rules.'

'I know. It's sweet of you to worry about me, Tony, but I'm a big girl – I can take care of myself,' she reminded him gently.

'In other words, I should mind my own business.

Okay, I can take a hint. You know where I am if you need me – bye.'

'Bye.' Maggie put the receiver back on its cradle gently. She *always* knew where Antony was if she needed him, bless him.

It wasn't late, yet Maggie felt worn out. The hotel was virtually empty and she had no plans for going out again. Deciding to indulge herself with an early night, Maggie left her office and made her way upstairs.

Maggie didn't think she would have to wait long for Jake to contact her after the previous night, but she hadn't expected to hear the sound of his motorbike on the gravel beneath her window the very next morning. Blearily, she reached for her bedside clock and groaned. It was barely eight o'clock.

A smattering of tiny pebbles hit her bedroom window, making her jump. Dragging herself out of bed, Maggie went to the window and, opening it wide, leaned out.

Jake was standing below, dressed in the usual jeans and T-shirt, his bike parked arrogantly in the middle of the driveway. He raised his eyebrows at her as he saw she wasn't dressed.

'What on earth do you think you're doing here at this unholy hour?' Maggie groaned.

Jake's eyes roved her dishevelled appearance, taking in the low cut of her nightdress, pulled tight across her breasts as she leaned out of the window. His face registered amusement, underscored by desire, and in spite of herself, Maggie felt an answering tug deep in the pit of her stomach.

'I'm taking the bike for a spin along the coast – I

thought you might like to come, seeing as how you're not exactly rushed off your feet around here.'

Maggie wanted to ask him how he knew that, but quickly decided it didn't matter. The early-morning sunshine promised a long, sunny day and it was true, she hadn't much to do. The thought of hitting the open road on the back of Jake's motorbike was very alluring and, following her impulses, Maggie nodded.

'All right. Give me half an hour to get dressed and I'll come down.

'Ten minutes,' Jake said firmly.

'Twenty – and you'd better still be waiting when I get outside.' Determined that her word should be the last, Maggie closed the window with a decisive slam.

After a lightning-quick wash, Maggie pulled out a swimming costume, a pair of cut-off denim shorts and a red cotton halter top. Covering up with an oversized white shirt, she ran a brush through her long hair, fastening it back at the nape of her neck with a bright red scrunchie. Rummaging around in the bottom of her wardrobe, she found a pair of chunky red plimsolls, barely worn, into which she pushed her bare feet.

They felt odd; she was too used to wearing high heels and the muscles of her feet protested mildly at the unaccustomed angle at which she was forced to walk. Catching a glimpse of herself in the mirror, Maggie grinned. Alexander would have a fit if he saw her dressed like this. It had to be the antithesis of the 'dressed for sex' look he liked her to follow.

It was curiously liberating, to dress for comfort instead. Though she had no doubt that sex was on the day's agenda, Maggie had a suspicion that it wouldn't matter to Jake if she was wearing a sack. It was what was underneath her clothes that mattered to him, his tastes were straightforward and, compared to Alex, relatively simple. Deciding that she couldn't be bothered with too much make-up, she dusted her face lightly with translucent powder and coloured her lips with the barest hint of lipstick before packing a shoulder bag with sun lotion, a collapsible sunhat and sunglasses.

Jake looked pointedly at his watch as she appeared in the doorway. Maggie laughed, feeling unexpectedly carefree.

'You can't complain,' she protested. 'I can't have been more than a quarter of an hour. What? What is it?'

Jake was watching her intently, his eyes scanning her features as she spoke.

'You look about sixteen in that get up,' he told her.

Maggie raised an eyebrow. 'Is that good, or bad?'

Jake's lips twitched slightly, as if he was struggling not to smile. 'Depends if you're going to buy your round at the pub, doesn't it?'

Maggie laughed and went to fasten the helmet he had brought for her. 'I thought you were offering sea and sun, not some dingy pub on the prom.'

Jake's face darkened. 'What makes you think I only hang out in dingy joints?'

Something in his voice betrayed his irritation and Maggie looked at him quizzically.

'No reason. Don't be so touchy.' She smiled to soften her words, but Jake did not return her smile. Instead he glanced at her broodingly before turning away and swinging his leg over the broad back of the bike.

Maggie followed suit, slipping her arms around his waist and feeling the taut, warm flesh beneath the thin cotton of his T-shirt. As soon as she was settled, he fired the engine and they drew away, sending up a spray of gravel in their wake.

Maggie clung onto him for dear life for the first half hour. It seemed to her that he went far too fast on the narrow, winding Cornish roads, taking risks that no one in their right minds should even think of taking as they rounded each corner.

Gradually, though, she became used to the motion of the bike and realised that he was, in fact, a more than competent rider, and she began to relax and enjoy herself. As they sped along, heading south, she had time to reflect on Jake's unexpected appearance outside her window that morning. His attitude towards her seemed to have softened, not enough to make her imagine for a moment that he had developed some kind of liking for her; his expression when he looked at her still held not a little contempt. But it was clear to Maggie that he saw more in her now than he had when they first met. Perhaps that would open up new possibilities for them.

After a good hour on the road, Jake turned down a narrow lane which led to a car park by a wide, sandy cove. Maggie felt her spirits lift with excitement as she took off her helmet and breathed in the fresh, ozone-laden air. Though she had lived and worked in Cornwall for almost a year, she had had little time to enjoy the more natural attractions the county offered. Now she felt as she had as a child, itching to feel the sand between her toes.

She turned and grinned at Jake. Her smile clearly dazzled him, for he raised his eyebrows, his mouth curving into an answering grin for the first time since she had known him.

'Come on,' he said irritably, as if embarrassed by his momentary lapse.

160

Nothing could dampen Maggie's happy mood as they climbed the sand dunes towards the summit. She cried out with pleasure as they reached the top and the entire beach lay spread out before them, the sea stretching to the horizon, a shimmering, glittering expanse of blue.

'Oh Jake – it's gorgeous.'

She was off before he could respond, running down the steep dune towards the virgin sand, her ponytail bobbing behind her. Maggie felt the warm breeze brushing her face and the sun, still climbing to its zenith, beating down on her unprotected head and she was reminded of her childhood. It was almost a surprise to remember that she wasn't carrying buckets and spades and a beach ball, that her brothers weren't streaking ahead of her, unmatchable, ready to hammer in the cricket stumps or dive straight into the freezing waves.

Jake followed at a more leisurely pace, standing at the base of the dunes and watching her as she danced across the sand. After a few moments she returned to him, laughing.

'It's been years since I was on a beach.'

'Why?'

His question brought Maggie up short. Why *hadn't* she had a holiday for so long?

'Well,' she replied slowly, her expression sobering, 'last year it was because I was setting up the hotel, the year before I was too busy . . .' she trailed off, thinking of Antony and Alexander and her complete immersion in their closed, claustrophobic world.

'And before that?' Jake prompted her.

Maggie shot him a sad smile.

'I was working. Building up my career. Maybe if

161

I'd known I was going to jack it all in I'd have taken it a bit easier. Made time to watch the grass grow.'

Jake dropped onto the soft, powdery sand at the base of the dunes and brought out two cans of beer from the holdall he had brought down with him. Handing one to Maggie, he pulled the tab on his and took a long swallow. Maggie did likewise. The beer was slightly warm, but refreshing nonetheless.

'Working's a mug's game,' he said after a few moments.

Maggie sat down beside him and took another swig from her can.

'Oh? So what do you do to keep body and soul together? Rely on the state?'

'I don't *rely* on anything. I look after myself, just like most people, if they've got any sense.'

'Okay – but how? Don't tell me you're a full time crook.' Maggie's voice was light, but she was very aware that she had just put into words one of the things that bothered her about Jake – his apparent lack of visible support. But if she had hoped to he enlightened, his next words disappointed her.

'I get by,' he said evasively, his eyes narrowing as he scanned her features. 'Why the interest?'

Maggie shrugged. 'Just making conversation.'

Jake's glance made it perfectly clear what he thought of that idea and Maggie shut up, concentrating instead on finishing her beer.

After a few minutes, Jake stood up. Maggie watched, squinting in the bright sunlight as he stripped off his T-shirt and began to unbutton his jeans. Underneath them he wore a pair of functional black swim shorts, neither too tight nor too baggy. Maggie ran her eyes over his near-naked body greedily.

162

Her fingers itched to smooth the matt of thick black hair which patterned his chest, arms and legs, but she held back, conscious that she was leaving herself open to rejection if she made a pass at him in so public a place.

She had barely taken any notice of their surroundings, but now she saw that two or three families had set up camp on the beach, as well as a large group of young people who, surrounded by their surfing paraphernalia, lounged around, waiting for the conditions to alter. Looking at the sea, Maggie wondered if they really expected to be able to surf. The waves were impotent, harmless ripples, gentle enough for there to be several children playing at the water's edge.

'I'm going to hire a board,' Jake told her, 'do you want one?'

Maggie looked at him in disbelief. 'Are you serious?'

A ghost of a smile flickered across his face. 'Rarely. Just a body board, Maggie, nothing too difficult.'

'But the sea is like a mill pond.'

Again, a small smile flickered across his features. 'The tide's due to change in a couple of hours. Well?'

Maggie imagined herself trying to stay afloat on a body board and smiled weakly. 'Okay.'

She watched him walk across the sand to the camper van which had set up shop at the far end of the cove. This wasn't what she had expected when Jake turned up that morning. A secluded cove, perhaps, or a lonely country lane where they would have fallen on each other and spent the day indulging in the wildest sex imaginable – that she could understand. But sunbathing, surfing – it was all so *normal*.

Maggie laughed softly to herself. Maybe it wasn't so bad. It could be fun. She could wait for the sex.

The day was long and lazy. Maggie dozed in the sun then swam for a while with Jake in the chilly water. The tide did change and she found herself shrieking and laughing with Jake and all the other surfers as she mastered the body board, half drowning herself in the process. At lunchtime Jake went off to fetch them something to eat. He arrived back with fish and chips drenched in vinegar which they ate out of the polystyrene trays, crunching sand and salt together.

Jake, though far from talkative, seemed more relaxed than Maggie had ever seen him before and she realised that she too was gradually uncoiling. Her hair stiff with sea salt and her limbs crusted with sand, she had never looked less like the sex queen she had become. For once her appearance didn't matter to her. There were no mirrors to catch her unawares and Jake's eyes, when they lingered on her, expressed nothing but appreciation.

The only fly in the ointment as far as Maggie was concerned was that, apart from responding to her request to rub sun oil in her back, a task which he had undertaken quickly and vigorously, Jake had not touched her. Not once.

Strangely, the fact that the man now lying next to her seemed disinclined to indulge in any deeper intimacy only served to make her want him more. It was late afternoon and most of the other people on the beach had begun to drift away, in search of showers, suppers and other distractions. Jake seemed to be in no hurry to follow them and Maggie lay beside him quite contentedly, listening to the sound of the waves and the occasional screech of the sea-gulls. She felt tired from doing nothing all day and curiously happy.

Levering herself up on to one elbow, she gazed at Jake's profile. He had a strong face with a good bone structure. His lips were thin and hard, the same colour as the rest of his face. With his eyes closed, masking his usual disdainful expression, he looked younger, more approachable.

Tentatively, Maggie reached out and traced the shape of his forehead, his nose and his jaw with two fingertips. Brushing them lightly over his lips, she was surprised when they parted and his tongue licked at her finger. Maggie looked down into his hard blue eyes and felt her stomach quiver.

'I thought you were asleep,' she said unnecessarily.

'So you decided you'd take advantage of me?'

Maggie laughed. 'Would you mind?'

Jake drew her fingertip between his lips and circled it with his tongue. The inside of his mouth was wet and warm and the sensation of his tongue moving across her skin made Maggie feel the same way.

'That depends,' he said, pushing her finger out of his mouth with the tip of his tongue.

Holding his eye, Maggie's hand hovered over his belly. Slowly, she lowered her wet finger and circled the ridge of skin around his navel.

'Why did you bring me here today?' she asked him as she stroked the tense abdominal muscles.

Jake stared at her, his expression unreadable. 'The truth?'

'Of course,' Maggie murmured, moving her hand lower to caress his thighs.

'I wanted to see if there was more to you than met the eye.'

Maggie paused, frowning. 'So what's the verdict?'

'We're still here, aren't we?'

'I see. Why did you think we might not be?'

Jake shrugged, covering her hand with his and moving it down to the soft bulge in his swim shorts. It hardened under her palm and Maggie stroked it, circling the outline of his glans with her fingertip.

'All you want is this.' Jake said, a tremor in his voice betraying his growing excitement.

Maggie smiled. 'A woman can like sex, can't she, without it being all there is to know about her?'

Without giving him time to reply, she dipped her head and brushed her lips along the now defined length of his cock. It felt warm and vital and she felt desire trickle through her veins, slowly, like warm honey.

Jake lay very still, making no attempt to stop her, yet not encouraging her in any way either. His eyes, when she raised her head to look at him, were opaque, his mouth unsmiling as she pulled down the straps of her swimming costume. She stood up, peeled it off, and kicked it aside. Picking up the white shirt lying on the sand, she pushed her arms into the sleeves, but left it open so that he could still see her nakedness. His eyes lingered on the exposed, depilated flesh of her mons and she allowed her feet to slide apart slightly on the sand.

She knew that he would be able to see the evidence of her arousal glistening on the darker-pink flesh of her labia. The inner lips peeled apart as she bent her knees and straddled him on either side of his waist. The sand felt warm and grainy as she sank onto her knees, her sex pressing against one of his tautly muscled thighs in an open-mouthed kiss of invitation.

Holding Jake's eye, Maggie ran the palms of her hands up from his stomach to the flat, hard planes of his chest. His body hair felt crisp beneath her fingers,

166

his nipples two flat, round discs of rubbery flesh, surrounded by thick, black hair.

'You have a wonderful body,' she told him truthfully, enjoying the feel of his flesh beneath her hands. 'So warm and strong and pliable.'

'Pliable?'

Maggie smiled. 'Under certain conditions.'

Jake's eyes narrowed, roaming appreciatively over her breasts as she leaned over him.

'Why don't you ever kiss me?' she asked him, bringing her mouth close to his.

He frowned. 'I kiss you,' he protested mildly.

'No you don't. You have never kissed me. Not mouth to mouth.'

'You've never looked as though you've needed resuscitating,' he said flippantly.

'I want you to kiss me.'

Her lips brushed lightly against his, her tongue tracing a ticklish path along the join. Jake lay motionless, unresponsive, his eyes staring into hers.

'I thought it was only prostitutes who didn't like kissing,' Maggie whispered, nipping lightly at his lower lip. 'Let me in . . .'

Drawing her tongue into a point, she used it to drill lightly at the corner of his mouth. She could taste beer and sea salt and the inner sweetness of his mouth; the combination left her feeling intoxicated. Allowing her upper body to dip, she moved the tips of her breasts provocatively across his chest. His hair rasped ticklishly against her nipples, teasing them into hardness.

Swaying, Maggie brought her pelvis into contact with his, fitting the now tumescent length of his shaft along the aching cleft of her sex. Slowly, she lowered herself until she was lying on top of him, thigh to thigh, sex to sex, nipple to nipple.

At the first full-length contact of her skin against his, Jake's lips parted on a gasp. Maggie struck at once, plundering the soft inner recesses of his mouth with her tongue, seeking out the sweetness within.

Once his defences had been breached, Jake's tongue met hers and parried with it, his lips moving, grinding against her teeth. The ferocity of the kiss took Maggie's breath away. Her heart hammered in her chest while her legs parted of their own accord, her labia moulding themselves around his lycra-covered shaft.

Suddenly impatient, she broke away, just for long enough to tear the swim shorts from him. His cock sprang free, firm and virile, and Maggie grasped it in her fist. Jake groaned as she moved her hand up and down its length quickly, several times, before rubbing the tip along the slippery crease of her sex.

'Wait.' Reaching for his jeans, he pulled out a condom and handed it to her. 'Use this.'

Maggie held his eye as she unwrapped it and positioned it over the bulbous head of his penis. Jake was breathing heavily, though his eyes gave nothing away. Maggie felt hot, feverish as she forced herself to unroll the condom slowly along the length of his shaft.

She wanted him with a need that bordered on the desperate. He had made her wait so long, spinning out the tension until she felt as if she would snap. Virtually oblivious now to their surroundings, Maggie straddled Jake, positioning his cock-head at the entrance to her body. The crash and hiss of the waves formed a background symphony to the tumult of sensation which rolled through Maggie's body as she sank down on him, impaling herself on the hard, unyielding spike of his penis.

'Oh God,' she whispered, her lips, hot and aching, fastening on his.

Jake lifted his hips, meeting her thrust for thrust as she moved on him. Maggie sat upright, leaning back until his penetration was so deep it bordered on the painful. Sweat pooled in the dip of her collarbone and ran in little rivulets between her breasts and down the sides of her body. Lifting his shoulders, Jake leaned forward to catch it on his tongue as it reached her belly. Maggie gasped as his tongue delved into her navel and swirled round it, tantalising nerve endings she never knew she had.

Twisting her hips from side to side, she ground down on him, welcoming the ripples of pleasure-pain which travelled from deep inside her womb up through her belly to her solar plexus. She felt breathless, disconnected from everything except the reality of their two bodies melding together, moving as one, in perfect harmony.

Maggie knew the exact moment when he lost control. His cock seemed to vibrate inside her, his back arching, his buttocks lifting up off the sand to meet her. His imminent orgasm caused a ripple effect, a kind of wave of sensation along the walls of her vagina which, in turn, triggered her climax so that when at last they came, it was together. Both cried out, clinging to each other, his sweat-slicked skin sliding against hers, his heart beating violently against her breast, matching the rhythm of her own.

'Jake,' she screamed, her voice carrying along the empty beach.

His hands ran up and down her back, as if he wanted to fold her over him, wanted her to consume him. Maggie held his head tightly against her breast. His mouth moved heatedly over her skin, his tongue circling her nipples, licking at the rapidly drying sweat between her breasts.

They peeled apart reluctantly. Gazing wordlessly at each other, they collapsed side by side on the sand. Maggie looked up at the sky, faded now to a denim blue, hearing the blood pounding in her ears as her heart rate gradually slowed and returned to normal. She didn't expect it to be Jake who broke the silence.

'I'm leaving next week.'

Maggie sat up and turned towards him. 'Leaving? What do you mean?' she asked, wondering why she suddenly felt so bereft.

'I thought I'd spend the rest of the summer in Europe.'

He was so calm, so nonchalant. Maggie struggled to achieve the same tone. 'What will you do?' she asked him, aware that she had failed.

To her surprise, Jake smiled at her. 'Do? Why are you so hung up on *doing*? When do you give yourself time to just *be*?'

Maggie stared at him. His philosophy of life was seductively simple and she found herself wishing that she could adopt it, if only for a little while.

'Take me with you.' The words were out before she had time to even realise she wanted to say them. Jake's eyes bored into her in the ensuing silence. Finally he sat up. Maggie watched him as he climbed to his feet and began to dress.

'Why?' he asked at last.

She shrugged. 'I don't know. So that I can get away from – from my life for a while.'

Jake began to pack up their litter and Maggie dressed in silence, aware that he was considering her suggestion. The more she thought about it herself, the more attractive the idea became. The thought of

170

simply taking off – there had to be a way to make it possible.

'It wouldn't work,' Jake said finally, dashing all her hopes.

'Why not?'

'You and me – we're too far apart.'

Maggie laughed. 'We weren't a few minutes ago.'

As one they turned towards the car park.

'It's not enough.'

Now that Maggie had thought of the idea of going away with Jake, she wasn't going to allow the subject to drop that easily. 'I don't see why not,' she protested. 'What do you mean?'

Jake sighed and Maggie had the impression that he was choosing his words with care. 'I admit, we have great sex. But travelling around Europe isn't going to involve nonstop screwing. We'd drive each other nuts by the end of the first week.'

'How do you know that?' Maggie said, offended.

'Look,' he turned to face her. 'I travel light. I have few possessions, fewer ambitions, my tastes are simple. Whereas you – ' he laughed. 'Hot shot businesswoman running her own hotel, not to mention her own private harem. You're a rich bitch, Maggie, who's feeling jaded. Your sort are two-a-penny.'

Maggie turned on him, eyes blazing. 'I'll give you two-a-fucking-penny! You – you snob, Jake Curran. Having money might make me rich, but it doesn't make me a bitch.'

'Oh? So how would you describe the way you treat me?'

'I don't know what you're talking about,' she retorted, feeling distinctly uncomfortable at the turn the conversation had taken.

'Don't play the innocent,' he scoffed. 'You use me.

171

Whenever you fancy a quick leg over you come looking for me.'

It was too close to the truth for comfort and Maggie reacted with anger. 'How dare you?'

'What's wrong? Isn't your bit of rough supposed have any feelings – no opinions?'

Puffing with exertion after scaling the face of the sand dunes, Maggie began to walk more quickly down the other side. It wasn't true, what he was saying, she was sure it wasn't.

'You've made your opinion of me perfectly clear, on more than one occasion,' she hissed.

'Like when?'

'Like every time you look at me. I can see the contempt in your eyes, You treat me like dirt.'

'You're lucky I can bring myself to service you then, aren't you.'

Maggie was speechless. She couldn't work out where this sudden argument had sprung from, let alone how the ugliness had crept in.

'Stuff you,' she growled, aware that she was pink with anger. 'I don't want to spend another minute with you, let alone go away with you. I'll get a taxi home.'

Maggie stomped past his bike, aiming a kick at the nearside wheel that reverberated up her shin. Gritting her teeth she ignored the pain and set off on foot towards the village they had passed earlier. She didn't turn round when he shouted after her.

'Maggie, Maggie don't be an idiot.'

She carried on walking when she heard him start up the engine and draw alongside her.

'Come on, Maggie – let me take you home.'

'I don't need anything from you, Jake Curran.'

'Don't be so childish.'

172

'Oh – piss off.'

That did it.

'Right. Just don't bother to come to me next time you have an itch that wants scratching.' He revved the engine.

'You need have no fear of that – it wasn't *that* good!' Maggie retorted waspishly.

'Bitch!' he spat as he pulled away.

'Bastard!' Maggie screamed, but her voice was drowned by the roar of his engine as he sped away.

Chapter Eleven

*L*ena watched Maggie watching the new 'waiter', Kokhi and bit her lip thoughtfully. Maggie had been very subdued since Lena had responded to her call earlier in the week to pick her up from the middle of nowhere.

Lena frowned at the memory. Maggie hadn't looked like herself in plimsolls, plain top and shorts. Lena had never seen her looking so unkempt, with sand in her hair, her face scrubbed of make-up, sea salt staining her skin. At first, Lena had feared that she had been attacked. Then she'd learned that she'd been with that man. The biker. What Maggie saw in that uncouth lout Lena could not even begin to imagine.

Her mind went back to the conversation she'd had with Antony on the day that Maggie had disappeared with the biker. He had phoned to speak to her, to discuss the adverse publicity the fires had attracted to the hotel. He hadn't sounded at all pleased when Lena told him that Maggie had disappeared. It had been Antony who had guessed who she would be with, if not where she had gone. And he had been right, Lena fumed silently. Maggie had been unable to hide it from her.

Antony was as worried as Lena about Maggie's relationship with the biker. He had even gone so far as to imply that he would be more than happy to know that Maggie had resumed her affair with Lena. He thought Lena was safe, a far more suitable partner.

Lena smiled to herself. He was right, of course. If Maggie would only come back to her, she could make her happy. Far happier than that lout, or any other man for that matter, could possibly make her. Lena wouldn't need to compete for her attention any more. There'd be no more fires and, together, they could build the hotel up into the kind of success it should be.

Carried away with this vision of domestic bliss, Lena hurried away to Maggie's private office. Closing the door firmly behind her, she went over to the desk and picked up the phone. Flicking through Maggie's roladex, she found the number for Antony's direct line and punched it in. It was Antony himself who answered.

He seemed surprised to hear from her, but his voice was friendly and Lena's confidence grew.

'I hope you don't think I'm overstepping the mark, it's just that I'm worried.'

'About Maggie?'

She had his interest now. Lena pictured him leaning forward in his seat, a frown pleating his forehead into lines of anxiety.

'Yes. You were right, you see, about the biker. But it's not really that I'm worried about.' She paused, giving him time to speculate. 'I hope you don't mind me talking to you like this?'

'No, no of course not. After all, we've both got Maggie's best interests at heart. Please – speak freely Lena.'

Lena sighed, as if she was still worried about betraying Maggie's confidence. 'We-ell . . .'

'I'm sure she'd do the same for you if the positions were reversed.'

Sensing that Antony's patience was rapidly wearing thin, Lena continued briskly, 'She just doesn't seem to be herself. I picked her up the other day – you remember the day you called? She seemed upset, totally unlike herself. Since then she simply hasn't been with it. She didn't seem to want anything to do with the Ladies' Club dinner on Tuesday and, as you know, we've got a hen party in tomorrow. We managed without her on Tuesday, but the hen party, well . . .'

'Is she really that bad?'

'I think so.'

Lena waited. The workings of Antony's mind were almost audible over the telephone wire.

'Do you think I need to come down?' he asked eventually.

'Well, I think it might help. If you could, that is.'

Antony seemed to come to a decision. 'What time does the hen party arrive?'

'Eight o'clock.'

'Right. There's a train which gets in at seven – could you organise a car to pick me up at the station?'

'Certainly. See you tomorrow, Antony.'

Lena put the telephone down, then she hugged herself. With Antony nudging Maggie in her direction and with the entertainment planned for the following evening, Maggie would be putty in her hands.

Looking at the guest list for the proposed hen party on Friday morning, Maggie was finding it difficult to concentrate. Her acrimonious parting from Jake had unsettled her, leaving her feeling dissatisfied. They had left so much unresolved and she knew that she didn't want him to go to France without talking to him again.

Gina breezed in at that moment, ready for her shift, and Maggie glanced at her speculatively. She had known Jake since schooldays, maybe she could shed some light on his behaviour.

'Come and look through this with me, Gina,' Maggie said. 'It's the agenda for tonight's entertainment. I'd like your opinion.'

Gina raised her eyebrows. It was normally Lena's job to discuss these things with Maggie, a privilege she guarded jealously. But Lena did not seem to be around this morning – come to think of it, Lena had been conspicuous by her absence for much of the past couple of weeks, since she had been hospitalised after the first fire.

Giving a mental shrug – it was none of her business if Lena chose to jeopardise her position at the hotel – she went over to look at Maggie's plans. She smiled when she saw the players chosen.

'Does Susie know she's to star in the floor show?' she asked.

'Not yet – why? Don't you think she's ready?'

Gina laughed. 'She's been champing at the bit. What role are you planning to give her?'

'The submissive one, of course. Marietta Dean, she's the bride-to-be who booked this outing for her friends, specifically asked for a little mild S and M. I thought that Derry would be ideal, given the response his cock usually gets when it's revealed.'

Gina's eyes gleamed. 'Mmm. And he's certainly no shrinking violet when it comes to showing it off. I see you've marked Kokhi down as an assistant.'

'I thought I'd broaden his experience a bit.'

'Good idea. So what's the order – food, floor show and take it from there?'

Maggie laughed at Gina's succinct summing up of the planned events. 'It's a tried-and-tested formula.'

'Right. I notice though that you've only put down the guys for the more private happenings.'

Glancing at her rosters, Maggie saw that Gina was right. 'Do you think we need women too? It is a hen party.'

'Yeah, but I happen to know a couple of the guests.' Gina pointed at two names on the list. 'These two both swing either way. And Mariella Dean is the closest thing I've ever known to a nymphomaniac.'

Maggie made a few notes. 'Thanks, Gina. Without your help I might well have completely mis-aimed the whole evening.'

Gina flushed with pleasure at the praise. 'Think nothing of it.'

'No, you've been a big help. I don't know what's the matter with me these days – I can't seem to concentrate on anything for long.'

Gina looked at her speculatively. 'It wouldn't be Jake Curran who's distracting you, would it?'

Having engineered the opportunity to talk about him, Maggie took a seat in the reception area and leaned forward confidentially. 'You tried to warn me about him, didn't you?' she said, injecting a rueful note into her voice.

178

Gina looked uncomfortable. 'Well, I – '

'It's all right,' Maggie interrupted her hastily, 'I appreciate your concern for me. It's only a shame that I didn't listen. Not really.'

Gina looked decidedly flushed and she seemed to be finding it difficult to meet Maggie's eye. Gradually, the truth dawned.

'You think more of Jake Curran than you're letting on, don't you Gina?' asked Maggie softly.

At first she thought the girl was going to deny it. Then she nodded, her eyes flickering up to meet Maggie's before sliding away again.

'Pathetic, isn't it? Jake and I, we used to be something of an item a few years back. When we met up again we seemed to virtually take up where we'd left off. Or so I thought.'

Maggie winced at the bitterness in the other girl's voice. 'What went wrong?'

'It was my mistake. I thought Jake felt the same way I did. Then I caught sight of his face when you discovered us in the cellar, and I realised he'd been using me.'

'Using you?' Maggie prompted when Gina fell silent.

'He set me up. He used me to get to you.'

Maggie stared at her for several minutes as the implications of what she had said sank in.

'Gina, does that mean that you were lying when you told me Jake was someone I should be wary of?'

Glancing at Maggie again, Gina's expression was wry. 'Not entirely. Jake's a heartbreaker, always has been. But that's all.'

Maggie sighed. 'Well, it doesn't really matter now anyway. He's leaving next week on an extended trip around Europe.' She hoped that only she could hear

179

the note of wistfulness which had entered her voice, but Gina must have picked up on something, for she unexpectedly took Maggie's hand and squeezed it. 'He's probably off on another assignment. That was half the trouble between us – I never knew if he'd turn up for a date, he was always dashing off somewhere.'

'Assignment? What sort of assignment?'

'Jake is a photographer. Didn't you know?'

A photographer? Every word of their argument came back to haunt Maggie. It had started with her worries about his lack of visible means and had escalated into a slanging match. Why hadn't he told her what he did for a living instead of allowing her to carry on thinking that he was some kind of petty crook? *Because he shouldn't have to explain himself* a small voice mocked her. She shouldn't have doubted him.

The conversation with Gina left Maggie feeling depressed. She was short with Lena when she passed her on the stairs and she decided that it would be a good idea if she rested a little before the guests arrived for the entertainment in the evening. She couldn't afford to allow her own personal problems to get in the way of her guests' enjoyment.

When she came downstairs again, an hour before they were due to arrive, a familiar figure was waiting for her in the lounge.

'Antony.' Crossing the room she kissed him on both cheeks, then stood back to look at him properly. 'What an earth are you doing here?'

He smiled the wide, disarming smile she knew so well. 'I spoke to Lena on the phone the other day and she told me about the evening you had planned. It sounded interesting so here I am.'

Maggie eyed him suspiciously. 'Are you sure you haven't simply come to safeguard your investment?'

'Maggie, I'm shocked. Don't you know I get lonely at the club on my own now that both you and Alexander have gone. I only need the slightest excuse to come down.'

'Hmm. Well, since you're here, I have something I need to do before the guests arrive. Be a dear and check the room for me – I shouldn't be more than half an hour.'

She walked away briskly and went outside to her car. Since Antony was here she might just as well make use of him. With him making the last-minute checks she was free to give in to the impulse to drive round to the estuary to speak to Jake. There wasn't time for anything else, but she hoped she could at least make it so that their parting was not on such bad terms.

To her relief, his bike was parked by the houseboat and the light was on inside. He came out on deck when he heard her car stop outside. It was only then that it occurred to her that he might well have another woman aboard and she suddenly felt rather awkward.

'Hello Jake.'

He didn't return her smile, nor did he invite her on to the boat. Instead, he strode across the gap between the boat and the bank. His long hair was loose and it blew in the early-evening breeze as he faced her.

'When do you leave?' Maggie asked him.

'Wednesday,' he told her, his eyes wary.

'Oh. I came to say goodbye. After the other day – well, I just wanted to say goodbye properly.' She turned away, discouraged by his lack of response.

'Maggie – '

'Yes?' Her heart lifted as she turned back again.

'It was a good day, wasn't it?'

She smiled. 'Oh yes. Can I ask you something? Gina tells me you're a photographer. Is that right?'

Jake nodded, looking at her quizzically.

'Why did you let me continue to think you were into something dodgy?'

Jake smiled faintly at her use of the word. Then he shrugged. 'You'd already made your mind up about me. I didn't want to disillusion you.'

There was a thread of hurt behind his words that made Maggie feel ashamed. 'I'm sorry,' she said. 'But there's one other thing that puzzles me. You called me a rich bitch. You said the main difference between us was that I had a great deal, while you had nothing. Yet knowing what I know now, I would have thought that our material worth was broadly similar.'

Jake's smile was bleak. 'I wasn't talking about pounds and pence, Maggie. I was talking about the baggage you carry around up here.' He tapped the side of his temple with his forefinger.

'I don't understand.'

'Possessions, material things, they mean something to you. I travel light, often living rough – I don't think you'd thought things through when you asked to come with me.'

'You're probably right. But I have since, and I'd still like to come.'

Jake shook his head. 'No, Maggie. There's still the hotel – have you thought of that? It ties you down.'

'I suppose it does,' she conceded. 'Speaking of which, I have to get back. Goodbye Jake.'

'Goodbye Maggie.'

He made no attempt to kiss her or touch her in any way at all, and Maggie felt inhibited about making the first move. Instead, she slipped back into her car and backed away, aware of him watching her until she was right out of sight.

Mariella Dean was small and dark with a wicked sense of humour. She was determined that her hen night would be one to remember and ensuring that her needs were adequately met had kept Maggie occupied when she got back to the hotel. It also distracted her from Lena and Antony, who appeared to have formed an improbable alliance where she was concerned.

'What went wrong between you and Lena?' Antony asked her when they sat down for dinner.

Maggie sighed. 'Tony you're so transparent – I can see right through you. Lena and I were never meant to last. She's far too possessive.'

Antony raised an eyebrow. 'You broke a golden rule by getting involved with an employee in the first place. It might not be so easy to break things off.'

Irritated, Maggie speared a forkful of seafood. 'I already have broken things off.'

Antony frowned. 'But I thought Lena said – '

'Ssh – Susie and Derry are going to get up in a minute.'

The lights in the lounge dimmed and the male singer who had been crooning softly in the back-ground as Mariella and her friends enjoyed their meal took a bow. There were a dozen women around the bride-to-be's table, all of them high on anticipation, their inhibitions broken down by alcohol and the general ambience of the hotel. An expectant hush descended as a soft spotlight fell on the raised podium in the centre of the room.

There was a general stir as Derry, dressed in black

183

leather trousers and a white shirt, strutted to the centre of the stage, a long lead held casually over his shoulder. The other end of the lead was attached to a ring on a leather collar. The leather collar was all that Susie wore and a shocked gasp went up from the hen-party table as she came into view.

'This, ladies,' Derry said in his soft Irish drawl, 'is Susie. Isn't she pretty?'

Unclipping the lead, he let it drop to the floor as he tipped up Susie's head and kissed her on the mouth. Susie stood absolutely still, though from where Maggie was sitting she could see that she was trembling with excitement.

'Susie has been a very naughty girl, isn't that right, Susie?'

Susie nodded and her blonde hair brushed her cheeks. Maggie recognised the glitter in her eyes as desire and knew she had been right to pick the girl.

'What must we do to naughty girls, Susie?' Derry asked, his deep voice caressing every woman in the room.

'Punish them,' Susie whispered.

'What was that? The ladies over there couldn't hear you.'

Glancing at Mariella's table, Maggie saw the way the women held themselves, tense with anticipation and she smiled to herself. She had managed to surprise them.

'You have to punish me,' Susie said, her voice high and clear this time.

'Punish you – that's right.'

Derry walked slowly round her, as if considering what her punishment should be. Every woman there shared Susie's tension as they waited for Derry to speak again. The room was so quiet Maggie knew that everyone would be able to hear a pin drop. All eyes were fixed on the naked, trembling girl in the spotlight.

Susie was fairly short and slender with clear, white skin. Her pubic hair was sparse, the same shade as her cornsilk-blonde bob, and her breasts were firm and high, reminding Maggie of two ripe apples. They were topped by the palest-pink areolae she had ever seen.

Derry put his lips against Susie's cheek from behind and said, 'What's it to be, Susie? The whip, or the crop?'

A muffled gasp came from the direction of Mariella's table, loud in the tense silence.

'Oh, please – the crop,' Susie replied fervently.

Maggie shot Antony a wry smile. She would have to teach the girl how to feign at least a little reluctance for the delectation of her audience.

Kokhi arrived on the stage carrying an ordinary leather-tipped riding crop with a small loop at the end. Knowing from experience how that loop would sting, Maggie felt a warmth spreading from the pit of her belly.

Taking the crop from Kokhi, Derry slapped it against the palm of his hand, standing back as he watched Susie.

'Prepare her,' he told Kokhi.

Kokhi produced a bottle of oil which he sprinkled liberally on to his palms. Quickly, he spread it across Susie's breasts, working it into the flesh until her nipples stood out like two swollen pips in the centre and her breathing was audibly ragged.

'Turn around please,' he said politely. 'Bend – touch your toes.'

Susie's bottom was rounded and fleshy, the skin

rippling as Kokhi oiled every centimetre with care. Looking around Maggie could see there wasn't a woman in the room who remained unaffected by the sight, or who didn't imagine Kokhi's long, sensitive fingers kneading her own buttocks.

'Enough,' Derry ordered.

Kokhi stepped back, but he didn't leave the stage.

'Turn so that the ladies can see your face – sideways.'

Still bending from the waist, Susie shifted round until she was presenting her profile to the audience.

'Up a little,' he said, tapping the underside of her breasts with the crop. 'Hands behind your head.'

Waiting until Susie had adopted the position he had engineered, Derry turned to the audience and smiled.

'Now ladies, you will be able to watch to see how much Susie enjoys her punishment.' He walked round and stood behind her so as not to obscure their view.

He passed the crop under Susie's face and, without having to be told, she pressed her lips against it. Every line of her body betrayed her tension. The room was thick with it, the atmosphere heavy with sexual arousal. A communal gasp went up as Derry flicked the crop against Susie's breasts. No one had been expecting that, least of all Susie who let out a little yelp of surprise.

Derry flicked the crop again and her breasts quivered, swinging slightly below her. The nipples stood out as two prominent beads, each an angry red after being touched by the crop. She kissed the crop again as Derry brought it to her lips, then he moved so that he was positioned by her upturned buttocks.

He looked over at Maggie, and she nodded at him. Earlier she had told him to keep the whipping light,

186

knowing that the main attraction of the evening was going to be his oversized prick when it was revealed to the audience. Glancing at his crotch she saw that his erection was growing very satisfactorily. She noticed that Derry's arousal had not escaped Antony's attention, either – he was watching the young man closely, a film of perspiration breaking out on his brow.

The thwack of the crop against Susie's bare buttocks was very loud in the silence of the room. One of Mariella's guests moaned quietly and Maggie saw that George, seeing her heightened tension, had gone to sit beside her. Susie's flesh shivered as Derry delivered three more controlled strokes to her now gently glowing buttocks.

Handing the crop to Kokhi after Susie had kissed it again, he began to unbutton his shirt.

'You can kneel down now Susie. You've taken your punishment so well I'm going to reward you.'

Maggie could sense the increase in the women's attention as Derry slowly stripped off his shirt before turning his attention to his trousers.

'Oh my God,' someone breathed as his cock sprung up, semi-erect, from the opening of his fly.

'Maggie – you never told me it was *that* big,' Antony whispered in her ear.

Maggie chuckled. 'It wouldn't have been fair,' she told him, her lips against his ear. 'I told you – Derry's strictly a ladies' man. You leave him alone.'

'What a waste,' Antony murmured as Derry removed the rest of his clothes and stood naked in the middle of the podium. His stance spoke of his pride in his body, every well-honed muscle held taut as he accepted the admiration of the women watching.

His penis was thick as well as long, its circumcised

187

head bulbous and smooth. Marietta Dean looked glazy eyed as she suddenly got up from her chair and stepped forward.

'Can I touch it?' she asked, provoking raucous laughter from her friends. 'Just to see that it's real.'

Kokhi gave Mariella his hand and helped her up onto the stage. She approached Derry cautiously, as if she was already regretting being so bold. He stood very still as, tentatively, she reached out her hand and stroked it. Immediately, it rose up, reaching full hardness in response to Mariella's caresses.

'It's real all right,' she told her friends.

She seemed fascinated by it, becoming bolder with her caresses as Derry stood patiently in front of her. After a few minutes, he caught her questing hand in his.

'Later,' he said, loudly enough for her friends to hear.

They shrieked with laughter and Mariella turned pink. Maggie frowned at Derry, warning him not to embarrass the girl.

'If you'd like to, that is,' he added courteously.

Marietta smiled and the awkward moment passed. As she climbed down off the stage, Maggie wondered fleetingly if this was what she'd had in mind when she'd requested a hen party 'with a difference'.

Meanwhile, Susie was waiting patiently for Derry to turn his attention back to her. Her lips opened wide as he nudged them with the tip of his massive penis. It was an incredible sight to see it disappear into Susie's stretched mouth, especially as she was so clearly enjoying the experience.

Kokhi knelt down behind her and began to fondle her tingling breasts. Susie closed her eyes, taking more of Derry's cock into her mouth.

'Open your legs,' Derry told her, sticking to the script even though his voice was thick with arousal. 'Kokhi will make you come.'

Susie shuffled her knees apart and Kokhi's hand slipped into the warm channels of flesh between them from behind. Maggie imagined the bliss of pressing her burning bottom against the cool silk of Kokhi's shirt and felt her own sex flesh moisten in sympathy.

Judging by the muffled sighs and gasps coming from Mariella's table, many of her friends had turned their attention away from the spectacle on the podium and were busy getting to know the 'waiters' the hotel had supplied to service them. One woman was sitting on George's lap, her long skirt concealing what they were doing. It was clear, however, from both her expression and that on George's face, that both were near to climax.

On the podium, Susie was coming already, her cries gagged by Derry's oversized cock, still moving in and out of her mouth. He withdrew slowly. The light showed up the glistening surface of his cock as he turned towards Mariella. As if in a trance, the would-be bride rose from the table and waited for him to come down from the stage. Unselfconsciously naked, his erection sticking out like a totem in front of him, Derry went to her and, taking her hand, led her from the room.

Kokhi picked the exhausted Susie up bodily and carried her from the stage, heading towards the staff quarters. All the women from the hen party, plus the smattering of individual guests who had opted to join the party, were now fully occupied with their respective partners. Antony turned to Maggie and the look of hot lust in his eyes sent a jagged dart of desire searing through her belly.

Lena appeared at her elbow just as Maggie was about to suggest they go up to her room.

'There's a phone call for you,' she said, her voice a flat monotone.

Maggie looked at her properly for the first time that evening. Lena looked lovely in a sophisticated cocktail dress in black, edged with jet beads. Her glorious red hair had been piled on top of her head, escaping in fronds around her face. She looked as though she had dressed to impress, and yet Maggie hadn't seen her in the room at all since the entertainment began.

'Who is it?' she asked, fully prepared to tell Lena to report that she was unavailable.

'Brett Tunnock.'

Her heart leaping, Maggie changed her mind at once. Standing up, she leaned over and gave Antony a peck on the cheek. 'Sorry, Tony. I'll leave you in Lena's capable hands.'

She smiled at Lena, who looked horrified at the suggestion. As she walked away, she heard Antony saying,

'Sit down, Lena, and I'll buy you a drink.'

Lena's eyes bored into Maggie's back as she hurried from the room to take Brett's call.

'Brett?' she said, picking up the receiver in her office.

'Hello Maggie. I hope I'm not interrupting anything?'

Maggie had forgotten how his voice sounded; deep and mellifluous, it set her nerve endings tingling.

'No,' she replied, 'nothing at all. I was beginning to think you were never going to ring me.'

His chuckle was low and rich. 'I'm sorry. It's just that when we make love I want to be able to give you the time you deserve. I've been working odd shifts. In fact, I'm on duty now.'

Already aroused, Maggie found the thought of Brett's lovemaking intensely pleasurable. 'I could come down to the fire station now,' she suggested.

Brett laughed. 'Shameless hussy. No, Maggie, I don't want a quickie up against a fire tender, I – .'

'Sounds like fun to me,' Maggie interrupted with a laugh.

'Another time maybe. Like I said before, I want the first time we come together to be long and slow. I want us both to savour every minute.'

His seductive voice was having a profound effect on Maggie. 'When do you go off duty?' she asked him, her voice husky with need.

'Six o'clock.'

Glancing at her watch, Maggie saw that it was already 2 a.m. She didn't feel in the least bit tired after her rest that afternoon. She knew she wouldn't be able to sleep anyway until she had eased the very specific ache which started in her womb and radiated through her, in ever increasing circles of lust.

'If I come down to the station, could I hang around until your watch ends? I wouldn't get in the way, and then I could go home with you at six.'

Brett was silent for a minute. When he spoke, his voice was thick with suppressed excitement. 'All right,' he told her. 'I'll leave the side door open – the men are mostly in the mess room. Try not to let them see you. My office is on the first floor, straight up the stairs. You can't miss it.'

'I'll see you in about an hour,' Maggie told him. She was so aroused she didn't know if she was going to be able to wait that long.

'I'll be waiting,' he promised.

Smiling to herself, Maggie replaced the receiver.

Chapter Twelve

*L*ena did not appreciate being dumped on Antony. But, knowing that it was imperative to hide her true feelings from him if he was to remain an ally, she gritted her teeth and made small talk for several minutes. When she could bear it no longer, she said, 'It feels kind of odd, chatting over drinks when people are fornicating all around us, don't you think?'

Antony grinned. 'A little bizarre, I'll grant you.'

'Do you want me to see if there's anyone free for you?'

She hid a smile as she saw that she had succeeded in shocking him. Perhaps in her desire to make it perfectly clear that she was not available herself she had been a little too blunt. She had to admit to a feeling of malicious satisfaction that she had clearly made Antony feel uncomfortable. His supreme self-assurance could be more than a little wearing at times.

'That's very kind of you, Lena, but I'm quite content,' he replied, a touch stiffly.

'If you'll excuse me, then?'

She rose and left him. The moment she turned her back on Antony, Lena forgot all about him. She was consumed by a need that no man could ever satisfy and she knew she would not be able to think straight until it had been assuaged.

When she had bathed and dressed for the evening she had harboured high hopes that she would be sharing her bed with Maggie again tonight. Lena had been certain that Maggie would have been turned on by Susie and Derry's performance, and that she would surely notice the effort Lena had made with her appearance – her indifference came as a body blow to her confidence. She refused to entertain the idea that when Maggie had told her it was over, that had been her final word.

In the event, though, Maggie had barely given her a second glance, and after she had heard that Brett Tunnock was on the telephone – well! Lena stalked restlessly through the ground floor, performing her routine checks as duty manager automatically, without really taking in what she was doing.

It didn't take her long to realise that Maggie had actually left the hotel. She'd left a message with the night receptionist and had gone without so much as a word of goodbye. Hurt slowly hardened to cold fury as Lena made her way to the staff quarters.

In her mind's eye, she could see Maggie meeting up with the craggy fire officer. Torturing herself with images of Maggie removing her clothes for him, offering him her lovely body, made her feel sick with jealousy.

As if her imaginings had been imbued with sound, Lena heard a muffled giggle from the room she was passing. She paused. It was Susie's room and the sounds coming from inside were unmistakably sexual. Lena recalled Kokhi carrying the exhausted Susie from the stage and smiled to herself. Relations between staff were strictly forbidden – it was one of the Black Orchid organisation's most uncompromising rules. A transgression generally warranted instant dismissal, and not many of the staff risked it. Most had little energy left over after looking after the guests anyway. Obviously, Kokhi and Susie, the two newest staff members, had not heeded the warnings.

With a wicked smile curving her lips, Lena tried the door to the room. It was unlocked. Such carelessness deserved to be punished, she told herself, slipping quietly into the room.

The couple on the bed were oblivious to everything except what they were doing. Susie was lying on her back, her hips raised by several pillows so that her pelvis was tilted upward. Kokhi was moving in and out of her, slowly, making it last. The lighting in the room was dim, but Lena could see the look of absorption on the young man's face as he eked out his control.

Quietly, her eyes feasting on the slender bow of Susie's arched body, Lena slipped off her panties and kicked them aside.

'So this is where you got to, Susie.'

The looks on the couple's faces as she spoke would have made Lena laugh if she wasn't so keyed up. Kokhi withdrew instantly, leaping to his feet and facing her with a look of sheer consternation. Susie scrambled into a sitting position and faced her.

'Lena, I – that is, we – '

'Save your breath,' Lena interrupted, holding up her hand. 'You know the rules, both of you. If Maggie or Antony hear of this you'll both be out of a job.'

'Oh, please don't tell them, Lena – it won't happen

again,' Susie pleaded. She glanced towards Kokhi who nodded his head vigorously.

'That's right,' he said, 'it won't happen again.'

'Are you suggesting that I should let this shocking transgression pass unpunished?' Lena feigned outrage, walking round the bed and glancing from one to the other as if trying to decide who was the most culpable.

She was enjoying herself. Both Susie and Kokhi looked at her in silence, their eyes following her nervously as she walked around the bed again. Susie had a hectic flush across her chest and neck and Lena realised she had been very close to coming. Excitement still shone in her eyes, despite the look of anxiety that Lena's arrival had put there.

'Miss Lena – I am to blame, not Susie.'

She turned at Kokhi's quietly spoken words, her eyebrows raised. Kokhi regarded her calmly, his erection undiminished in the face of her scorn.

'How very gallant,' she mocked. 'Sorry, Kokhi, no can do. It's the high jump for both of you. Unless . . .' she allowed her voice to trail away, relishing the look of hope which flared in their eyes before she dashed it. 'But no, I couldn't possibly allow that.'

'What, Lena?' Susie said, as Lena had known she would. She leaned forward eagerly, waiting for Lena to elaborate.

Slowly, Lena removed the pillows that had been under Susie's hips and rearranged them against the headboard. Her eyes never leaving Susie's, she sat on the bed, settling herself comfortably against the pillows. Understanding dawned on the other girl's face as Lena opened her legs to reveal her naked, freshly shaved vulva.

'I don't mind Kokhi fucking you,' she said conversationally, 'so long as it's from behind and doesn't interfere with the real business in this bedroom.'

For a moment she thought that Kokhi was going to object, but a look from Susie silenced him. It wouldn't matter if he had objected, Lena thought to herself as she watched Susie get into position. It didn't much matter to her whether he went or stayed. Though it did give her the most delicious view of Susie's fleshy bottom as he raised her hips and sank his cock back into her sex.

Lena sighed as Susie burrowed her head between her thighs and set to work on Lena's tender flesh. She found her clitoris with her tongue and began to nibble and lick at it, like a cat at a bowl of cream. Lena knew she wouldn't forgive Maggie for this latest humiliation, but Susie was making a good job of making her forget, for a while. Closing her eyes, Lena leant back on the pillows and surrendered herself to pleasure.

The fire station was eerily quiet as Maggie let herself in by the side door and crept up the metal stairs. The tap of her high-heeled sandals sounded overloud and she tried to walk on the balls of her feet. As she passed a door on the landing she heard the low murmur of voices and guessed this must be the mess. Moving quickly past for fear that someone might come through the door, she made her way right to the top of the stairs where Brett had his office.

He was sitting at his desk, in his shirt sleeves, writing a report. Maggie had a few brief seconds to study him before he saw her. She saw that he looked fit and tanned, but tired, as he had when he had attended the second fire at the hotel. Without his bulky, protective clothing, she could see the definition of his body and she felt a small mule's kick of desire deep in her stomach.

Part of the thrill of this escapade was, she knew, the idea of finding her pleasure outside the hotel and the club, just as she had with Jake. Although Brett didn't move her in the same way as Jake did, what he was offering her was a respite from her usual sexual routine and she was looking forward to the experience. She liked Brett and she knew from the way he kissed her in his office that he would be an accomplished lover. For once, Maggie decided, she would lie back and let a man make love to her, without any effort on her part. Her skin tingled at the thought.

Brett looked up as she entered and smiled at her. 'I wasn't sure that you'd come,' he said, striding across the room and taking her into his arms.

Maggie tipped her face up for his kiss, clinging to him as he bent her back slightly over his arm. The kiss left her feeling breathless, aching for more.

'I said I'd come,' she pointed out when she had recovered. 'I always do what I say I'm going to do.'

Brett smiled and went back round his desk. 'You said you'd hang around here until I finish, then come home with me,' he reminded her.

'Yes. And I will,' she said.

'I have to finish this report. There are magazines in the rack under the coffee table – help yourself.'

His eyes mocked her gently and Maggie realised that he fully expected her to grow bored within half an hour and go home again. Flashing him a challenging smile, she went over to the couch which sat against one wall of his office and rummaged under the coffee table for something to read.

She could feel Brett's eyes on her bottom, moulded by the flimsy jersey fabric of the dress she had

197

changed into and she took her time, hoping the sight was disconcerting him. She'd worn the dress deliberately, because she guessed it would be the kind of thing he would find attractive. Though it was a 'look-at-me' red, it skimmed rather than clung to her figure, its skirt falling in soft swirls to her mid-calf. It was a modest dress, almost demure apart from the colour, and the way it moved around her figure as she walked.

He would be able to tell that she wasn't wearing any underwear by the way the fabric clung. Sitting down on the couch, Maggie slowly crossed one leg over the other, deliberately giving Brett a flash of tanned thigh as her skirt rode up her legs before she smoothed it back down again.

The magazine she had picked up soon bored her and she leaned forward to put it back and look through the stack for another one. Near the bottom there were several copies of a soft-core girlie magazine. It had been years since Maggie had looked at one of these and she picked it up out of idle curiosity.

Glancing at Brett, she saw that he was pretending to be absorbed in the report he was writing. From the tension apparent in every line of his body, she guessed that he had noticed what she had picked up and was finding it difficult to look as if he hadn't. She smiled to herself as she opened the pages.

Acre upon acre of naked flesh sprung from the page, the colours vivid, drawing the eye. Maggie recoiled from the 'in your face' photography – gynae shots of pouting, wet-lipped women invariably sucking a forefinger as they stared into the camera with dewy, lambent eyes. She closed the magazine with a small sound of disappointment.

'I didn't know that was there,' Brett said, looking up from his report as she put the magazine away.

Maggie regarded him sceptically. 'Really?'

'Honestly. You look shocked – I'm surprised at you, Maggie. I thought you'd be more open-minded.'

Maggie laughed aloud. 'I am about what I do. But to me what's in that magazine is a distortion of what sex should be about.'

'How so?'

She had all his attention now, she noticed. He swivelled in his chair so that he was facing her, the report he was so keen to finish lying forgotten on his desk. Maggie picked the magazine up again and flicked thoughtfully through the pages, aware of Brett's eyes trained on her face, as if gauging her reaction.

'I know men's sexual psyche is more attuned to the visual than most women's, but in my experience there's room for a wider range of stimuli than this.'

Turning the magazine around, she showed Brett a photograph of a woman sitting, knees bent and apart, spreading the lips of her sex with her fingers. Brett's expression was unreadable as he looked from it to Maggie. She glanced at the photograph again before closing the magazine and putting it aside with a grimace of distaste.

'That looked like an anatomy lesson,' she said.

A ghost of a smile flitted across Brett's features.

'They never had anatomy lessons like that when I was at school.'

'Thank God they didn't – what a warped view of womankind to present to an adolescent of either sex.'

'So – what do you suggest would improve it?'

Maggie smiled slowly. Her eyes never leaving Brett's, she said, 'I would treat my male readers with

199

a little more respect. Acknowledge that they're capable of more than just a knee-jerk reaction...' keeping her voice deliberately smoky, Maggie allowed the fingers of one hand to drift across her breast, circling the areola with the very tip so that the skin puckered and hardened.

'I'd have a long, slow build-up, to entice the reader to linger over each and every photograph.' She transferred her attention to her other breast, cupping its fullness in her palm and squeezing, almost absently, her thumb brushing the hardening tip. 'Maybe a striptease, revealing the model's body inch by beautiful inch.'

'But you'd still end up with what's in there in the end,' Brett pointed out reasonably.

'Yes – but it would make more sense. Have more impact.'

The Adam's apple in Brett's throat moved as he swallowed and she knew that she had thoroughly unsettled him. *That'll teach him to expect to be able to ignore me in favour of a report*, she thought triumphantly, knowing that she was being childish, but not able to give a damn.

'Anyway,' she continued, taking her hand away from her breast and picking up a copy of an angling magazine, 'you carry on with what you were doing. I don't want to be a distraction to you.'

From beneath her lashes, she watched as Brett tried to do as she had suggested. He couldn't concentrate, and after a few minutes Maggie saw that he laid down his pen with a grimace of disgust.

'How long is it until you go off duty?' she asked him, her voice low and husky, infinitely seductive.

Brett glanced as his watch. 'Just over an hour,' he said.

200

'Is there a lock on your door?'

Catching her drift, he raised his eyebrows, but did not get up from the desk. 'Long and slow. That's what we agreed, and that's what I'm hanging out for.'

Maggie pouted, her eyes dancing with amusement. 'Are you *sure* you can wait that long?' she teased him, uncrossing and re-crossing her legs.

Brett groaned. 'Yes – I can. I have to attend a debriefing. Will you be all right on your own?'

'Of course,' Maggie replied, watching him as he stood up and took his jacket off the back of his chair. The fabric of his regulation trousers was stretched tight over his crotch. She hoped that fatigue and the necessity for routine would not diminish it entirely before she got him home.

'Would it be all right if I had a look round?'

Brett looked doubtful as he put on his jacket.

'I won't touch anything,' she promised.

'All right. I'll meet you back up here in half an hour, OK?'

Striding over to her he bent and kissed her, full on the lips, taking her by surprise. His mouth was firm and warm on hers and, by the time he broke away, Maggie was trembling.

'*Touché*,' he murmured, his eyes roving her face and the hectic flush which had crept into her cheeks. 'Now we both have something to think about.'

Maggie watched as he strode away, aware that her heart had quickened in her chest. She hadn't been one hundred per cent certain why she had come tonight, whether because she had strong feelings towards Brett, or simply because she knew he would be able to occupy her thoughts, thus directing them away from Jake. It didn't really matter. He wanted her; she wanted him. It was all refreshingly simple.

After a few minutes, Maggie got up and went to look around the fire station. Although the whole place was flooded with light, there was a quality to the silence which she knew she would only find at this hour, just past dawn. From the walkway she could see that there were two fire engines below, both equipped ready for action. At the end of the walkway there was a round hole cut into the metal, wide enough for a large man to slide down the fireman's pole.

As a child, Maggle had always wanted to try this method of descending quickly downstairs. Glancing around her, she reassured herself that she was alone before kicking off her shoes and wrapping herself round the metal pole. Clinging on for dear life, she slipped slowly down the pole, conscious of the smooth metal rubbing against the front of her body, setting up a wonderful friction between her legs. She hadn't realised quite how much she had turned herself on whilst in the process of teasing Brett until she felt the easing of tension caused by the slow, sensuous slide.

At the bottom, she stood for a few moments, still pressed against the pole. It would not take long to bring herself to a climax by rubbing herself against it, but she decided that she would save that first orgasm for Brett. The anticipation was excruciating, but she knew that a little self-control now would pay dividends in the very near future.

Wandering around the tenders, both looking very large now that she was on the ground floor with them, Maggie eyed the reels of hose and imagined them being pulled slowly between her legs. She winced at the lewdness of the thought, running her fingers along the shiny paint of the fire engine as she made for the stairs.

Retrieving her shoes, Maggie resisted the temptation to take a second trip down the pole. Instead she sat down and waited impatiently for Brett to come back up to the office.

'Ready?' he asked her as he returned to the room at last.

'Oh yes,' Maggie smiled. 'I'm more than ready.' Smiling, she walked over to Brett and put her hand in his.

Brett lived in a stark, sixties-style flat overlooking the sea. Its furnishings were of the type that is found in rented accommodation, though Maggie barely noticed her surroundings at all as they were hardly through the door when Brett started kissing her again.

Knowing that now there were no restrictions, no outside constraints to stop them, added an urgency to their love-making that thrilled them both. Until now they had only been able to snatch the odd kiss in Maggie's office or Brett's – now there was no chance that anyone was about to walk in on them, all the barriers had been removed.

His fingers were warm against her bare skin as he slipped them under her long hair to caress the nape of her neck.

'Maggie, Maggie,' he murmured against her throat as he steered her through the living room and into the bedroom.

Sinking down on to the bed, Maggie was aware of the pink streaks across the early morning sky outside and she was glad that Brett made no attempt to close the curtains. They were high, about six storeys up, and there was nothing opposite but the sea and sky.

She stretched, like a cat in the sun, watching Brett through narrowed eyes as he undressed. Removing his jacket, tie and then his shirt, he was silent as he watched Maggie watching him. His chest was broad and muscular, only lightly furred with hair which, as he moved and the light shone through it, Maggie saw was beginning to take on a tinge of grey. The long, hot summer had perfected his tan and his skin glowed bronze, smooth and healthy. Maggie imagined how it would feel and sat up on the bed, trembling with anticipation.

Brett dispensed with his trousers with an economy of movement which Maggie admired, removing his socks at the same time. Underneath he was wearing plain black cotton boxer shorts which barely contained his erection. He left them on as he sat on the bed next to her and ran his fingers through her hair.

'I've been waiting for this,' he told her, his eyes on her lips as she replied,

'So have I.'

Reaching for him, she ran her hands over his shoulders and down his arms. His skin felt like warm silk. Placing one hand over his heart, she felt it pound against her palm and her own pulse quickened. She could smell the sharp tang of fresh male sweat as he folded her in his arms and her head swam dizzily. He was so big, so solid. There was something very primitive about being clasped against his chest and Maggie's body responded at once.

'Let me take off my dress,' she murmured against his hair, 'I want to feel your body against mine.'

Brett helped her to pull her dress over her head, his eyes widening in delight as he saw that she wore nothing at all underneath it.

'God, you're beautiful,' he breathed, his lips

moving against the tender place behind her ear. 'But you're moving too fast.' He pulled back, holding her face in his hands and staring deep into her eyes. 'Nice and slow – remember. I want it to last.'

'It doesn't have to be only once,' Maggie protested half-heartedly. Her heart was hammering in her chest, the adrenalin pumping through her veins making her feel jumpy. There was so much tension in her she felt she might snap.

Brett did not smile, though his eyes shone. 'I want to touch every inch of you with my fingers, with my lips. By the time you leave I want to know your body so well I could draw a map for the Ordnance Survey series.'

Maggie laughed and his eyebrows rose.

'You think I'm joking? Turn over.'

Eyeing him quizzically, Maggie rolled on to her stomach, watching him over her shoulder as he reached into a drawer in the bedside table and took out a bottle of oil. She gasped as he unscrewed the top and, holding the bottle high, he dribbled it across her back.

'Lie down,' he said. Gentle fingers smoothed her long hair to one side and Maggie closed her eyes. Arousal churned through her, hot and impatient, and she tried to calm it, to match Brett's slow, steady pace.

The bed dipped as Brett straddled her, one knee on either side of her hips as he began to work the sweet-smelling oil into her skin. Maggie groaned involuntarily as his fingers dug deep into her muscles, dissolving the tension in her back until she felt boneless, incapable of independent movement.

The silence in the room grew thick with tension as Maggie's body grew more and more fluid. Brett's fingers were firm and sure, but Maggie could swear that there was electricity in their tips as he gradually shifted his attention to her bottom. It was bliss to lie with her cheek against the cool pillow while Brett oiled her buttocks and the back of her legs, right down to the soles of her feet.

'Roll over,' he said from the end of the bed, a gruffness in his voice which betrayed the effort such self-control was costing him.

Maggie moved very slowly, rolling on to her back and easing herself up the bed so that her head was propped on the pillows. Her eyes followed his hands as they massaged the oil into her feet and between her toes, almost tickling her, his touch just firm enough to make it pleasant. She sighed as he circled her ankles and began to work up her thighs.

Raising her arms above her head, Maggie settled back on the pillows as Brett's oily fingers neared the junction of her thighs. The folds of flesh still hidden by her closed legs were swollen and moist and Maggie could already feel a dull pulse beating at the apex of her labia. If he touched her there, now, she knew she would come.

Brett didn't touch her there. Instead, when he reached her groin he turned his attention to her arms. Maggie gasped as his hands, slippery with oil, smoothed the skin in the dip of her armpit before sliding easily up her arm to her elbow. Once he reached her wrist, he lifted it and brought her arm down gently.

'Mmmm – where did you learn to do that?' Maggie moaned as he began to manipulate each finger in turn.

'I had a girlfriend once who was a beauty therapist,' he told her.

'And she taught you how to massage?' she asked as he turned his attention to her other hand.

'Caroline liked to receive as well as to give,' he explained.

'Fair enough. I can see why too – you must have been a quick learner.'

'I practised a lot.'

He pressed his lips against the corner of her mouth, teasing it into a smile with the very tip of his tongue.

'Really?' she whispered, her heart pounding as she contemplated where he would spill the oil next. So far he had paid minute attention to every part of her except those areas that would drive her wild: her breasts, belly and the soft, melting folds of flesh between her thighs.

Sitting up, Brett smiled down at her. Maggie caught the wicked gleam in his eye and shivered.

'Oh!' she gasped as he spilled oil over her breasts. It ran in little viscous rivulets from the tip of her nipples down over the mounds of her breasts and pooling in the valley between them. It was into this cleft that Brett passed the palms of his hands, pressing gently so that Maggie felt she would melt into the mattress.

For a few moments he ignored the aching peaks of her breasts, so that when, at last, he began to stroke and knead them, they quivered with suppressed delight. Maggie felt her nipples harden still more and was compelled to allow her thighs to roll apart slightly to ease the pressure on her sensitive vulval flesh.

Brett saw the movement and smiled at her. Bending his head he caught the very tip of one nipple between his lips and nibbled on it, sending little shock waves of pleasure down from her breasts to her mons.

'Uh-oh, that's so-o good,' she moaned, writhing against the sheets as his hands moulded her waist and hips, his thumbs brushing across the taut plane of her stomach. 'Please, lower . . .'

Brett chuckled softly and dipped his head to place a wet, open-mouthed kiss at the top of the naked crease between her labia. Maggie gasped. She had expected him to oil her shaven mons too, maybe even to work the oil into her already dew-soaked skin before sliding himself into her. She hadn't expected him to begin this slow, leisurely exploration with his lips and tongue.

Under pressure from his tongue, she felt her labia open to him, the intricate folds of flesh peeling apart, eager for the touch of his lips inside each secret channel. Brett licked and sucked at her swollen flesh as if he was tasting the juiciest, most exotic fruit. Carefully avoiding the little promontory of her clitoris, Brett teased and tantalised every inch, drawing a series of involuntary sighs and moans from Maggie's lips.

She felt his tongue wiggle into the elastic-walled channel of her vagina and she shifted her hips, wanting to feel him deeper, firmer. Her fingers ran restlessly through his thick crop of hair, her knee moving caressingly against the thick shaft of his penis, pressing against his boxer shorts. She wanted that inside her instead of his tongue and she moaned incoherently, trying to communicate her need.

Brett lifted his head and gazed down at her, his eyes lambent with desire. His fingers fumbled with the fastening to his boxer shorts and he drew them down, flinging them carelessly aside as he straddled her.

His penis was not particularly long, but it was

thick, solid looking, its foreskin already drawn back, the glans smooth and shiny. Maggie felt an atavistic fluttering in the pit of her belly as she imagined it entering her. The long massage and tantalising oral stimulation had left her with every nerve tingling, aching for satisfaction.

Reaching for him, she enclosed him in her hand and stroked the silky skin which moved over the steel-hard core.

'I want you,' she said, her eyes boring into his, 'now.'

Brett sat back on his heels and pulled her into a sitting position. Lifting her at the waist, he reversed their positions so that he was lying on his back, his head towards the end of the bed, and she was straddling him, her sex poised above the strong, straight staff of his cock.

As she sank slowly down on to him, Brett pulled himself up, holding her in his arms so that her breasts were crushed against the hard wall of his chest and her pubic bone ground against his.

They sat like that, very still, for a few seconds. Maggie could feel the breadth of his cock stretching her internal walls, giving her a feeling of fullness that sent ripples of pleasure through to her womb. Slowly, he began to rock her, so that he was moving inside her.

Maggie could see her own face reflected in his eyes as he moved forward to kiss her. The pace was slow and gentle, and yet somehow they managed to maintain the tension. It gained momentum as they moved as one, in silence, rolling so that Brett was on his back, then over again so that he was on top of Maggie.

A fine film of sweat made their skin stick then slip. Maggie felt as though a slow-spreading fire had started at the point where their two bodies joined and was sweeping gradually through her, consuming her with heat. Breathing seemed difficult and her heart-beat became faster as Brett began to move more deeply in her, thrusting now with increasing urgency.

'Ahhh,' Maggie let out her breath sharply as an orgasm took her by surprise. Without any kind of direct stimulation, the bundle of nerve endings in her clitoris could take no more. The silky, cleated walls of her sex convulsed around Brett's moving penis, setting up a chain reaction along its length so that, in no time, he joined her, tipping over the edge with an impassioned cry of release.

They clung together for a few moments, Brett's lips roving across Maggie's heated face and neck as he muttered endearments. Afterwards, they lay side by side, the duvet pulled up around their necks. The daylight streamed in through the uncurtained window, but neither were in any state to notice. In his sleep, Brett turned towards Maggie and drew her in close to him.

She lay, warm in his embrace, for several minutes. She felt as if her arms and legs had suddenly become impregnated with lead, they were so heavy. So were her eyelids and, within minutes, Maggie was also sound asleep.

Chapter Thirteen

*I*t wasn't until much later that they stirred. Maggie opened her eyes to find Brett's staring into hers.

'Well hello,' he said.

Maggie smiled, snuggling contentedly against him. She still felt sleepy and was disinclined to move from the rumpled comfort of the bed.

'Hello yourself,' she muttered, pressing her lips into the dip where his collarbones met.

'Can you stay?' he asked her.

'Hmm?'

'I said, can you stay?'

Maggie lifted her head with difficulty so that she could see the travel alarm clock on the bedside table. It was ten o'clock in the morning.

'Probably not,' she admitted, smiling. 'But if I ring the hotel I should be able to arrange cover for myself, if you're free that is?'

Brett sucked gently at her left ear lobe. 'I'm free all day.' The words held such an undertone of sensual promise that Maggie shivered.

'Pass me the phone,' she said, trying to ignore the effect of the progress of his lips down one side of her neck.

It was Lena who answered the telephone at the hotel.

'Lena? It's me. Is everything all right?' Maggie smothered a giggle as Brett caressed the sensitive area where her neck and shoulders joined with his lips.

'We were worried about you. When will you be coming back?'

Lena's voice seemed to be coming from far away and Maggie had to struggle to concentrate as Brett began to fondle her breasts. She could feel his erection, hard and straight, pressing against her spine as he pulled her closer to him.

'I'll be another couple of hours yet,' she told her.

'Maggie – '

'I'll talk to you later, Lena,' Maggie interrupted her, replacing the receiver and turning in Brett's arms to meet his embrace full on.

Lena stared at the telephone, the empty tone still buzzing in her ear. Maggie had hung up on her. She had actually hung up.

'Is everything all right, Lena?' Gina asked from the doorway.

Lena turned on her, unable to hide the strength of her feelings, allowing her fury to show. 'Of course everything's all right! Why the hell shouldn't it be?'

Gina held up her hands. 'Whoa, steady up, Lena. I just thought you looked as though you might have had some bad news or something, that's all.'

'Well I haven't, so you can go and get on with whatever it is you're supposed to be doing and stop poking your nose in where it doesn't belong.'

Turning her back on Gina, Lena blocked out the other woman's muttered response as she beat a hasty retreat. Damn Maggie and her fire officer! He'd been there with Maggie, Lena knew it. She had heard the noises, the breathy little gasp. Did Maggie think she wouldn't know what those noises meant? God knows, she had heard them often enough when Maggie was with her to know that she was in the middle of something.

Agitated, she leapt up from her seat and paced the room. Her anger and hurt burnt like a small flame in the centre of her chest, making it difficult to breathe. Her fingertips tingled, the way they always did when she was angry or upset and she knew that there was only one way she could bring herself back under control.

No – she would not. She could not. Not this time. She had started two fires at the hotel already, it was only luck that had shielded her from detection. Her intention hadn't been to start a fire, at least, not the first time. The garden shed was different, but as it was well away from the hotel, Lena knew that hardly counted. But that first time, supposing it went wrong again and Maggie found out what she had done. Lena groaned and wrapped her arms around herself. Maggie loved her, she knew she did. She just didn't realise how much, not yet.

Gulping air through her mouth, Lena swallowed back the sobs that were threatening to engulf her. She felt small, very small, vulnerable and alone. Without the flame to make her powerful she felt as though she might fade away altogether.

She started as someone knocked on the open door.

'Lena? Are you ill?'

213

It was Susie, hovering in the doorway as if afraid to come all the way in.

'I'm fine,' Lena snapped, pulling herself together abruptly. 'What is it?'

'Gina asked me to give you these.' She handed Lena the guest lists and the agenda for a party scheduled three days later.

Lena took them and nodded curtly at Susie. 'Thank you.'

She waited until the other girl had left the room before spreading the information out on Maggie's desk. Lena knew she couldn't go on like this. It would make her ill if she had to live with this endless stomach-churning insecurity. When Maggie got home she would confront her, make her see that the way she was behaving was hurting both of them. She'd *make* her see this time. Once and for all.

Brett shuddered as his climax overtook him, holding Maggie's hips still as his entire body seemed to convulse. Maggie, exhausted already, collapsed over him, her arms twining round his neck as they rolled apart.

'I thought men were supposed to slow down as they got older?' she teased him mildly when she recovered her breath.

Brett flashed her a warning glance, but there was laughter in his eyes. 'It depends on the woman,' he told her, his hands stroking the velvet soft skin of her belly.

Unlocking the embrace, they lay side by side in contented silence for a while. It was Maggie who stirred first.

'I suppose I'd better make a move,' she said reluctantly. 'May I use your shower?'

'Help yourself.'

His eyes followed her as she walked, unselfconsciously naked, across the bedroom and out into the corridor. The bathroom was next door to the bedroom and amply stocked with towels. Maggie stepped under the blissfully warm shower and began to soap herself down with the shower gel she found on the shelf inside the shower cubicle. It smelled of fresh pine needles and made her skin tingle.

There was a cotton robe on the back of the door. After towelling herself down, she put it on, realising at once that it smelled of Brett. It was a very masculine scent, very evocative of its originator and Maggie's now somnolent sex flesh pulsed gently in response.

Walking barefoot out of the bathroom her nose twitched as she recognised the smell of frying bacon. Following her nose, she turned away from the bedroom, towards the kitchen. Brett was dressed in jeans and an open-necked shirt the colour of the summer sky. He was barefoot, whistling softly under his breath as he cooked them both a full English breakfast.

'Mmm – I hadn't realised I was so hungry.' Maggie said as she came up behind him and slipped her arms around his waist.

He turned and smiled at her. 'Go and sit on the sofa while it cooks.'

'Thanks.'

Maggie sank into the unexpectedly lumpy sofa by the window, leaning forward to read the spines of the books on Brett's book shelf. They seemed to consist mainly of travel books and titles on photography. *A Cornish Odyssey* caught her eye and she pulled it off the shelf. She almost dropped it when she saw that it was by Jake Curran.

Opening it, she flicked slowly through the glossy pages, admiring the artistry of the photographer. Spectacular scenes of cliffs and surf, thoughtful studies of faces and small details that had caught his attention – even to her inexpert eye, the pictures were more than just competent. Knowing the man who had been behind the camera when these photographs were taken gave Maggie an inexplicable thrill. It was as if, through his photographs, Maggie could see the things he had seen, through his eyes.

'They're good, aren't they?'

Maggie looked up in surprise as Brett appeared in front of her with two laden plates. She had almost forgotten he was there in her absorption with Jake's photographs. She put the book aside carefully and took her plate from Brett. He passed her a tray and a knife and fork and sat down beside her, tucking into his breakfast with relish.

'He's a local man, isn't he?' Maggie commented as she too started eating.

'Curran? So I believe, yes.'

'I know him. It must be wonderful to have a talent like that – something you can share with other people. It's like allowing others inside your head.'

Brett glanced at her. He must have seen something in her expression for he paused and regarded her quizzically. Maggie could not explain why she felt the need to talk, to confide in someone, normally she was a very private person. But she sensed in Brett a sympathetic listener and the urge to talk about Jake was strong.

'Jake's going away next week, probably to take photographs for another book, in Europe. I want to go with him.'

'What about your job, and the hotel?'

Maggie grimaced and shrugged. 'I seem to have lost the enthusiasm recently. Oh, I don't know, Brett. Maybe I'm just ready for a change.'

'So what's the problem?'

Maggie smiled. 'Who says there's a problem?'

'If there wasn't, you'd be sitting there and saying goodbye to me because you were about to leave Cornwall with Jake Curran, you wouldn't be talking vaguely about being ready for a change.'

'Hmm. Well, for a start, it's not that simple. If I was to leave the hotel there would be arrangements that would have to be made, all of which would take time. And Jake isn't so sure that he wants me to come.'

'Ah. Well that is something of an obstacle,' Brett said, mopping his now empty plate with a slice of bread and butter. 'Any particular reason?'

'He thinks I wouldn't be able to hack it. You know – sleeping rough, travelling light. He feels I'm too materialistic, that I'd miss the lifestyle I have here.'

'And would you?'

'Possibly. Probably. But I know that I'm not content with my life as it is – I'd like to try something different.'

Brett regarded her thoughtfully and she smiled at him.

'What?'

'Nothing. I was just thinking that it's not as if it would be forever, would it?'

'No. Nothing is forever,' she replied softly.

They swayed towards each other, their lips meeting in a kiss that was tender rather than sexual.

'I'd better be going,' Maggie said as they broke apart.

'I don't suppose I shall see you again?' Brett asked as Maggie reached the door.

She looked at him, so handsome, so solid, so utterly decent, and she felt a momentary pang of regret. 'I suppose not,' she said softly. 'Thanks Brett.'

'For what?'

'For talking to me. You've helped me to sort out a few things that were muddled in my head.'

'Glad to have been of service,' he said with a small, self-mocking bow. Then he grinned and Maggie knew she was leaving him as she would want – with only pleasant memories of her.

Blowing him a kiss, she went to the bedroom where she dressed hurriedly. There was something she wanted to do before she went back to the hotel.

It was a relief to find Jake's houseboat moored in its usual spot on the estuary, even though she was disappointed to find that that was not at home. After a moment's debate, Maggie decided to leave him a note.

The boat swayed alarmingly as she clambered inexpertly over the side. Inside, everything was neat and tidy so that it didn't look nearly as cramped as it might. It felt curiously empty and unlived in, though, and Maggie had an uncomfortable feeling that she was intruding, violating Jake's privacy. Casting her eyes around the interior, she suddenly noticed a photograph stuck to the side of the refrigerator by a magnet shaped like a ladybird.

It was of a woman, her face in profile as she strode away along the path which followed the cliff top from the estuary to the Black Orchid Hotel. Her long, dark hair was blowing out behind her like a streamer and she was unsmiling, clearly unaware that the photograph was being taken. Recognising herself, Maggie felt an unidentifiable fluttering in the pit of her stomach.

That Jake had taken the photograph, never mind attached it to the side of his fridge, gave Maggie a warm feeling that she found she rather liked. It proved that he was not nearly as indifferent to her as he had led her to believe.

Maggie no longer felt as if she was trespassing and she did not fear any more that she was pushing him too hard. Rummaging in her bag for a pen, she ripped a lined sheet out of her Filofax. She wrote:

Jake, Sorry to have missed you. It wouldn't take me long to organise things here so that I could meet up with you on the continent. Please consider it. I think we could have some good times together. Maggie.

She paused, then added a kiss and left the note between the magnet and the photograph he had taken of her.

Whatever Jake decided, Maggie mused as she drove home, she would leave the hotel anyway. It was fortuitous that Antony was there at the moment; she would be able to talk to him about it over dinner this evening. Antony would be sad about her decision to pull out of their business partnership, but he would understand. At least, she hoped he would.

Maggie wasn't sure what she would do if she didn't go with Jake, but she was convinced now that it was time for a change of scene and to find a new challenge to excite her. That decision made, she felt quite light-hearted as she swept up the driveway to the hotel. She was totally unprepared to be met by Lena, standing, unsmiling, in the foyer.

'Hello Lena,' she said, surprised to find her assistant on the front desk at this time of day.

'Where have you been?' Lena hissed, her unusually pale face flushing with anger.

'I beg your pardon?'

'You've been out all night and half the day, leaving the hotel to run itself while you're fucking that Neanderthal creep – '

'Lena!'

'You're nothing but a cheap whore, a slut, a – '

'That's enough.'

Maggie's voice was icy enough to cut into Lena's tirade. She stopped speaking, her mouth half-open as if the words had been trapped in her throat and were merely waiting for an opportunity to burst forth and escape. Lena stared at Maggie through wild eyes and for the first time Maggie felt a tremor of fear. The other woman looked deranged, completely unhinged as she glared at Maggie. Her entire body was trembling with fury and her hands were clenched into fists.

'Lena – for Christ's sake!'

Maggie grabbed her hand and pulled her rigid fingers away from her palm, one by one. There were traces of blood where her long fingernails had pierced the skin. Lena continued to stare at Maggie, as if in a trance. She seemed to be oblivious to the pain which must have been caused by the wounds to her hands.

Suddenly, without warning, she pulled her hand away from Maggie's and smeared her open palm down one side of Maggie's face, streaking her with blood. Taken by surprise, Maggie recoiled, screaming, as Lena went for her with her other hand, fingers curled into claws, flailing and scratching.

Maggie was struck by how strong the other girl

220

was, and for a second she thought she would not be able to fight her off. From the corner of her eye she saw Antony running across the lawn towards them, and the knowledge that help was at hand, gave her new strength.

The two women fell to the floor, wrestling in a silent battle of wills until, at last, Antony pulled Lena away and held her fast.

'What the hell's going on? Christ, Maggie – your face,' he said, his voice rising in alarm as he saw the blood. 'Are you hurt?'

Maggie shook her head, unable to speak for the moment.

'Then perhaps someone will tell me what's going on.'

'Ask her,' Lena screamed, pointing at Maggie, who was struggling to get her breath. 'Ask her where she's been. Go on – ask her.'

'That's it,' Maggie said when she was able to speak. 'I've had enough – you've gone too far this time, Lena. Pack your bags and get out of this hotel. You're fired.'

For an instant, Lena looked stunned, then she seemed to crumple. Tears poured down her cheeks as all the fight went out of her. She slumped against Antony who had to support her as she pleaded with Maggie.

'Don't do this, Maggie. Don't you understand? I love you, only you, Maggie. I'd do anything for you.'

'So you've demonstrated,' Maggie snapped, wiping the smears of blood from her face with the clean handkerchief Antony handed to her.

'I didn't mean to hurt you, Maggie, truly I didn't,' Lena cried, her voice turning into a whine as she realised that Maggie was serious about sacking her.

221

'Just go, Lena.' Suddenly Maggie felt incredibly weary. She didn't want to even look at Lena. How on earth had she ever allowed herself to become involved with her in the first place?

Realising that Maggie was not about to change her mind, Lena turned to Antony.

'Please . . .?'

Antony shook his head. 'Maggie's right, Lena. You should go.'

Lena looked from one to the other of them, her now dry eyes shining, unnaturally bright.

'All right,' she said, belatedly trying to gather her dignity about her. 'But please let me sleep in my room tonight. It's already two o'clock; by the time I finish packing it'll be too late to find somewhere for the night.'

Maggie looked as if she was about to refuse, but just then a hotel guest wandered through the lobby, watching them with curiosity.

'That seems reasonable,' Antony said hastily. 'Provided you stay in your room, Lena, and leave first thing in the morning.'

'All right.' Lena would have agreed to anything at that moment, so long as she was to be allowed to stay the night. Turning away from them, she walked towards the stairs, aware of their eyes following her.

'How did this happen?' She heard Antony ask, but she was too far away to catch Maggie's low-voiced reply.

She'd show them, she vowed fiercely. She'd make them see how wrong they were to turn against her like this. And she'd make them sorry. Very, very sorry.

* * *

222

'What do you mean – you're leaving?' Antony said, his wine glass halfway to his lips.

They were sitting in the conservatory extension to the dining room where they had been served dinner, at Maggie's request, away from the guests and other staff. She hadn't anticipated that Antony would take this well and she wanted the privacy to explain.

'I can't help the way I feel, Tony,' she said, willing him to understand. 'All this craziness with Lena – it's the result of things getting out of hand. Of me getting out of hand.'

Antony still looked stunned as he placed his wine glass carefully on the coaster by his plate.

'Have you spoken to Alexander about this?'

Maggie knew that this would be the hardest part. 'No,' she said softly. 'This has nothing to do with Alex.'

Antony's eyes reflected his sadness at her quiet assertion. They both knew that there was far more to Maggie's effective resignation from the hotel than a simple dissolution of a business partnership. Without Alexander's input and approval, Maggie's decision meant the end of their quixotic personal relationship too.

'Maggie, are you sure about this?' Antony sounded close to tears.

Maggie nodded. 'I've given it a tremendous amount of thought. Since Alex went away – well, you know me, Antony. I always was less disciplined than you.'

'I ought to whip you for even thinking that you can leave us,' Antony said, his voice low.

A dark thrill shivered through Maggie and she nodded. 'Perhaps you should,' she said.

For an instant, Antony looked taken aback, then his eyes darkened and Maggie knew she had him hooked.

223

They rose from the table as one and, without a word, walked together to her room. Once inside, Maggie turned and faced him. It had been a long time since they had played the heavily ritualised games with which Alexander had guaranteed their loyalty. Now she found she craved the kind of release that she could only find in submission.

Antony's hand trembled as he unbuckled his belt and pulled it slowly through the belt loops. Maggie stood very still in the half light, her eyes following the movement of his fingers as he curled the leather belt around his hand.

'Pull up your dress,' he told her, his voice flat and emotionless.

Maggie understood how he felt and guessed he was acting on automatic pilot, barely able to comprehend what he was doing. A dozen images chased themselves through Maggie's memory, all of the times that the three of them, Antony, Alexander and herself had been together. Often, it seemed, the satisfaction they had achieved together had involved the ritualistic humiliation of either Antony or herself and yet she could not remember a time when she had felt more loved, more alive.

Thinking of things they had done together made her wet now, her sex readying itself, as if possessed of its own memory, knowing that the kiss of the belt on her upturned rump would be but a precursor to the most intense pleasure.

Slowly, without a word, Maggie pulled her dress up, over her hips and held it there. Antony's glance flickered over her naked mons and flat stomach and she saw a pulse begin to beat in his jaw.

'Turn around.' His voice was hoarse.

Maggie turned, aware of the way her own heart was hammering in her chest.

'Kneel on the floor by the bed,' he instructed.

Maggie did as she was asked, conscious of the soft scratch of the carpet under her knees as she took up the requested position. Everything seemed to have taken on an exaggerated manner, from the sound of the soft shuffle of Antony's shoes across the carpet to the feel of the duvet cover against the soft, exposed skin of her belly. As he paused behind her, Maggie lay her cheek against the cool fabric and raised her bottom in the air.

The first stroke took her by surprise and she gasped as the leather stung her buttocks. A familiar warmth swiftly spread through her and she rose up to meet the second blow. She needed this, she thought frantically, she deserved to be punished for daring to break away. And it felt so very, very good.

'Ahh.'

Antony was not hitting her hard and Maggie felt that his heart was not in it. Maybe he thought that by asserting some sort of dominance over her tonight, he would be able to keep her here until Alexander arrived to deal with her himself. Maggie welcomed the third stroke of the belt, as if by submitting to it she was in some way atoning for the fact that she was about to regain control of her own life. At the fourth stroke there was a warm rush of sensation through her and, to her surprise, she came.

Antony dropped the belt and knelt down beside her on the floor. His hand was gentle on her hair as he stroked it, turning her face towards him as he spoke.

'You weren't supposed to do that,' he said softly.

Maggie was surprised to feel the wetness of tears

on her cheeks. 'I know,' she said, her voice trembling. 'I think that demonstrates why I feel I have to go. Alexander can't control me any more, Tony. I never did submit as totally as you. And now I don't want to be controlled by anybody but myself.'

Antony stared into her eyes for a few minutes. He looked as though he might argue with her further, but he must have seen the determination in her eyes, for after a moment more, he nodded.

'You get some sleep now, Maggie. We'll talk in the morning.'

She smiled, not attempting to rise as he walked to the door. He smiled back at her from the doorway, sadness and regret apparent in every line of his body. On an impulse, she said,

'Can't you stay? Just for this last time?'

Antony looked tempted, but he shook his head. 'I can't. You know I can't. I belong to Alexander, body and soul. He wouldn't want me to sleep with you now.'

'I understand,' she whispered. 'Goodnight Antony.'

'Goodnight, Maggie.'

He touched his fingers to his lips and blew her a kiss, then he was gone.

Maggie dragged herself up and went through the motions of preparing for bed. It had been an exhausting day and she was glad that it was over. Now that she had told Antony her decision, she felt curiously numb. Not happy, nor even particularly sad any more, just numb. Once in her nightdress she plaited her hair into a single braid and slipped between the sheets.

Lying wakeful beneath the comforting blanket of darkness, Maggie reviewed the time she had spent under Alexander's spell and concluded that she had no regrets, neither about her involvement and participation, nor about her decision to leave. Her only real regret was that Antony would be lost to her. But then, he was never really hers in the first place, he was only ever on loan to her from Alex.

Alexander was the love of Antony's life. For him he would walk through a wall of fire without flinching. That he loved Maggie too she had no doubt, but it was a different kind of love, in a totally different league to the love he felt for Alexander.

She thought of Brett and the brief time they had spent together. Would she have wanted to make a future with Brett, or a man like him if she hadn't experienced life with Antony and Alexander? Maggie didn't know. Turning her thoughts towards Jake and the freedom he had come to represent, her heart gave a little flip. Would he respond to the message she had left for him on the boat and take a chance on her?

Yawning, Maggie rolled over and pulled the covers up to her chin. She was so tired. So very, very tired.

She woke up with a start. Disorientated, she grabbed the alarm clock by the bed and saw that she had been asleep for two hours. Straining her ears to try to detect the sound which must have woken her, it took her some minutes to realise that it was not a sound that had disturbed her at all, but a smell. The smell of smoke.

'Oh my God,' she whispered as the significance of the smell gradually sank in. That the hotel was on fire was difficult enough to believe, that it was serious this time was more so. And from the look of the black smoke now billowing beneath her door, the fire was already very, very close to her room.

Chapter Fourteen

M aggie leapt out of bed and ran to the bathroom where she soaked a towel and rolled it into a sausage shape before using it to plug the gap between the door and the floor.

At that moment the hotel's smoke detectors picked up the signals and the alarm began to sound through the sleeping building. From her window, Maggie could see the guests and staff beginning to congregate outside in the car park, just a trickle of them at first, then a flood. There was surprisingly little panic and Maggie felt a curiously detached sense of satisfaction that her staff were able to act in so responsible a fashion. She could see George and Derry trying to organise the guests into manageable groups whilst the night receptionist conducted a head count. There was no sign of Lena, so Maggie guessed she had taken her dismissal seriously.

Antony approached George and she could see them both gesturing. As they turned their attention towards her window, Maggie threw it open and waved frantically.

'Maggie – get out of there.'

'I can't.' she shouted back, 'the fire's right outside my door.'

She recognised the concern on Antony's face as he stood beneath her window. 'Okay – stay by the window. The fire brigade should be here any minute now, they'll get you out.'

'What about the guests?'

'Gina's checking now, but we think that everyone's out,' he reassured her.

'And the staff?'

There was a momentary pause before Antony replied. 'Everyone's safe, except . . . '

'Yes?' Maggie prompted impatiently as his voice trailed away.

'Lena's missing.'

Maggie found pictures running through her mind, like a film reel, of the first fire at the hotel, the one where Lena had been hurt. She felt again the sense of panic and prayed fervently that the other girl was safe. Much as she wanted her to leave the hotel, she bore her no ill will and the thought of her being trapped, as she was, made Maggie's stomach plummet.

'Wasn't she in her room?' she called down.

Antony shrugged. 'No one seems to know. Stay put, Maggie – help is on its way.'

'Well, I'm hardly going to be moving anywhere, am I?' Maggie muttered under her breath as she watched Antony stride back to the guests.

Checking behind her, she saw that the smoke was beginning to seep through the flimsy barrier of the towel and she ran to soak another before laying it alongside the first. Her door was hot to the touch and she guessed that the fire was right outside. How long would it be before the door gave way?

Realising she was still dressed in her nightclothes, Maggie pulled a pair of jeans and a jumper out of her wardrobe and dressed quickly. She began to cough and she realised that her best bet was to stay close to the open window. As she reached it, she heard the wail of the sirens and saw two fire tenders hurtle into the driveway, closely followed by a police patrol car and an ambulance. Between them their sirens created a cacophony of sound that, at that moment, was music to Maggie's ears.

Antony ran to meet them and she saw that he told the man in charge at once that she, and possibly Lena, were trapped in their rooms. Maggie's heart lifted as she recognised Brett and she waved, eager to attract his attention. While his men unreeled their hoses and set to fighting the fire, Brett had one tender brought close to the building and the ladders rose and extended until they were just below her window.

It was Brett himself who climbed up to rescue her.

'Am I glad to see you,' Maggie said fervently as he reached her window.

'Come on, Maggie – climb out on to the ledge. We have to get you out of here, and fast.'

Something in the tone of his voice alerted her to the urgency of the situation and Maggie began to tremble violently as she pushed the sash window up as high as it would go.

'Don't look down,' he cautioned her as she began to climb out through the window.

Glancing down at once, Maggie realised why he had told her not to. Though she was only on the first

230

floor, the ground seemed an awfully long way away and it spun crazily as she looked down at it. It took an effort to pull herself together and allow herself to be enclosed by Brett's waiting arms. Scooping her up, over his shoulder, he carried her down, apparently without any effort on his part at all. Maggie clung to the reassuring breadth of his shoulders and silently blessed the day she had met him. Frightened though she was, the minute she had recognised Brett she had felt safe.

A paramedic was waiting for her at the bottom with a blanket which he wrapped around her shoulders.

'Thank you,' she mouthed to Brett as she was led away. He nodded in a brief acknowledgement before turning away to join his men.

Whilst trapped in her room, Maggie had been afraid for her own safety, but she had not been able to visualise the full extent of the fire. Now, from the ground, she saw that the blaze had taken hold. The hotel had become like a giant furnace, the heat unbearable even from the spot on the lawn where she was led by the ambulance personnel.

Maggie stood and stared in horror The night sky was lit up with vicious orange streaks of light. Surely no one could still be sleeping in the hotel this dreadful night? Antony came to join her and she leant into him, glad of the warmth of his arm around her shoulders.

'Is everyone accounted for?' she asked him.

'All except for Lena. They're looking for her now.'

They did not speak any further, for there didn't seem to be anything more to say. Aside from the worry about Lena which was naturally at the forefront of their minds, they were both aware that they were powerless to do anything but watch as their hotel, the venture over which they had sweated and worked, burned away before their very eyes.

'To think I was going to leave the hotel,' Maggie said after a while, 'and now it has left me.'

Antony squeezed her shoulder in a small gesture of understanding and sympathy. Then Maggie felt him stiffen.

'Look,' he said, pointing to one side of the hotel.

They saw Lena, escorted by two police officers, coming towards them. Relief that she was clearly unhurt soon gave way to bewilderment as Maggie saw that her wrists were handcuffed in front of her.

'What's going on?' Maggie demanded as the small group reached them.

A uniformed police officer stepped between her and Lena and held up his hand. 'Stay back please, Miss.'

'But – '

'Stay here, Maggie,' Antony whispered.

'But Lena . . .?'

Lena stared straight ahead, giving no sign that she had heard Maggie. Her eyes held a curious blankness which made Maggie shiver. Lena looked as if she was in shock, her eyes opaque, her expression oddly flat. As if there was nothing but emptiness behind them.

Maggie watched as she was led away and put into the back of the patrol car, which was driven away from the hotel at speed.

Antony strode over to the second police car and spoke with the officer who was watching the blaze. Maggie frowned, annoyed that he had taken such a high-handed approach, telling her to stay put while he found out what was going on. Then she remembered that she was now Antony's partner in name only until the appropriate papers were drawn up, and she forced herself to let go.

Brett joined her while she was waiting. 'Are you all right?'

Maggie nodded. 'And you?'

'No major casualties. It could have been much worse. I'm only sorry we couldn't save your hotel, but the fire had already taken a hold when we arrived. It looks as though several small fires were set in various different locations, with the intention of destroying the entire building.'

'It *was* arson then – you've no doubt?'

Brett regarded her with compassion. 'There's always room for doubt,' he told her.

Antony rejoined them, looking grim. 'Lena has confessed to starting the fire.'

'*What?*'

'Apparently she's got a record as long as your arm. She's a regular pyromaniac.'

'But – why? What about the other fires – surely not!' Maggie could barely comprehend the implications of what Antony had just told her. How could it have been Lena who had been starting the fires?

'I must get back,' Brett said, breaking into her whirling thoughts.

'Yes. Thank you, Brett.'

'You seem to be thanking me rather a lot just lately,' he said softly so that only she could hear.

Maggie managed to smile, watching him walk away with a sense of farewell. Antony stretched wearily, glancing across to where the firefighters were now bringing the blaze under control.

'Thank God for insurance,' he muttered under his breath.

Maggie saw that what was left of the hotel was too far gone to be salvaged. 'Will it have to be demolished?' she asked him.

'It looks like it. What a way for it to end.'

'You'll build it up again, Tony,' Maggie said, squeezing his arm. 'You and Alexander, together.'

Gazing down into her upturned face, Antony bent his head and kissed her, gently, on the lips. Maggie smiled.

'I'll always love you, Antony,' she whispered.

'I know. And I you. What will you do now?'

'I –'

Maggie broke off as she recognised another sound, coming closer. Turning, hardly daring to hope, she saw Jake's motorbike coming to a halt at the end of the driveway. He sat there, the engine labouring, making no attempt to come any further.

'Go on,' Antony whispered. 'Follow your heart. I'll deal with what needs to be done here.'

Flashing him a grateful smile, Maggie gave him one last hug. She passed him the blanket which was wrapped around her shoulders, and began to run along the driveway. Jake stood up and removed his helmet, catching her in his arms. His eyes roved her face, and she saw his concern for her, unspoken, in their depths.

'I'm all right,' she whispered.

His mouth came down to cover hers in a kiss that was more eloquent than any words. When they broke apart they were both smiling. Without a word, Jake passed her his spare helmet and helped her fasten it under her chin. Swinging her leg over the pillion, Maggie hugged his waist, feeling the motorcycle engine throbbing under her thighs.

Jake pulled away, accelerating quickly, leaving the

hotel behind them. Maggie's spirits soared. She knew
this was a taste of the months to come and she pressed
her cheek against Jake's shoulders. She did not look
back, not once.

WE NEED YOUR HELP . . .
to plan the future of women's erotic fiction –

– and no stamp required!

Yours are the only opinions that matter.

Black Lace is the first series of books devoted to erotic fiction by women for women.

We intend to keep providing the best-written, sexiest books you can buy. And we'd appreciate your help and valued opinion of the books so far. Tell us what you want to read.

THE BLACK LACE QUESTIONNAIRE

SECTION ONE: ABOUT YOU

1.1 Sex (*we presume you are female, but so as not to discriminate*)
Are you?

Male	☐
Female	☐

1.2 Age

under 21	☐	21–30	☐
31–40	☐	41–50	☐
51–60	☐	over 60	☐

1.3 At what age did you leave full-time education?

still in education	☐	16 or younger	☐
17–19	☐	20 or older	☐

1.4 Occupation _____

1.5 Annual household income
    under £10,000 ☐   £10–£20,000 ☐
    £20–£30,000 ☐   £30–£40,000 ☐
    over £40,000 ☐

1.6 We are perfectly happy for you to remain anonymous;
but if you would like to receive information on other
publications available, please insert your name and
address

_____

_____

_____

_____

SECTION TWO: ABOUT BUYING BLACK LACE BOOKS

2.1 How did you acquire this copy of *The Black Orchid Hotel*?
    I bought it myself ☐   My partner bought it ☐
    I borrowed/found it ☐

2.2 How did you find out about Black Lace books?
    I saw them in a shop ☐
    I saw them advertised in a magazine ☐
    I saw the London Underground posters ☐
    I read about them in _____
    Other _____

2.3 Please tick the following statements you agree with:
    I would be less embarrassed about buying Black
    Lace books if the cover pictures were less explicit ☐
    I think that in general the pictures on Black
    Lace books are about right ☐
    I think Black Lace cover pictures should be as
    explicit as possible ☐

2.4 Would you read a Black Lace book in a public place – on
a train for instance?
    Yes ☐   No ☐

SECTION THREE: ABOUT THIS BLACK LACE BOOK

3.1   Do you think the sex content in this book is:
     Too much   ☐   About right   ☐
     Not enough   ☐

3.2   Do you think the writing style in this book is:
     Too unreal/escapist   ☐   About right   ☐
     Too down to earth   ☐

3.3   Do you think the story in this book is:
     Too complicated   ☐   About right   ☐
     Too boring/simple   ☐

3.4   Do you think the cover of this book is:
     Too explicit   ☐   About right   ☐
     Not explicit enough   ☐

Here's a space for any other comments:

SECTION FOUR: ABOUT OTHER BLACK LACE BOOKS

4.1   How many Black Lace books have you read?   ☐

4.2   If more than one, which one did you prefer?

4.3   Why?

SECTION FIVE: ABOUT YOUR IDEAL EROTIC NOVEL

We want to publish the books you want to read – so this is
your chance to tell us exactly what your ideal erotic novel
would be like.

5.1 Using a scale of 1 to 5 (1 = no interest at all, 5 = your
ideal), please rate the following possible settings for an
erotic novel:

Medieval/barbarian/sword 'n' sorcery ☐
Renaissance/Elizabethan/Restoration ☐
Victorian/Edwardian ☐
1920s & 1930s – the Jazz Age ☐
Present day ☐
Future/Science Fiction ☐

5.2 Using the same scale of 1 to 5, please rate the following
themes you may find in an erotic novel:

Submissive male/dominant female ☐
Submissive female/dominant male ☐
Lesbianism ☐
Bondage/fetishism ☐
Romantic love ☐
Experimental sex e.g. anal/watersports/sex toys ☐
Gay male sex ☐
Group sex ☐

Using the same scale of 1 to 5, please rate the following
styles in which an erotic novel could be written:

Realistic, down to earth, set in real life ☐
Escapist fantasy, but just about believable ☐
Completely unreal, impressionistic, dreamlike ☐

5.3 Would you prefer your ideal erotic novel to be written
from the viewpoint of the main male characters or the
main female characters?

Male ☐ Female ☐
Both ☐

5.4 What would your ideal Black Lace heroine be like? Tick as many as you like:

Dominant	☐	Glamorous	☐
Extroverted	☐	Contemporary	☐
Independent	☐	Bisexual	☐
Adventurous	☐	Naive	☐
Intellectual	☐	Introverted	☐
Professional	☐	Kinky	☐
Submissive	☐	Anything else?	☐
Ordinary	☐	_____	

5.5 What would your ideal male lead character be like? Again, tick as many as you like:

Rugged	☐		
Athletic	☐	Caring	☐
Sophisticated	☐	Cruel	☐
Retiring	☐	Debonair	☐
Outdoor-type	☐	Naive	☐
Executive-type	☐	Intellectual	☐
Ordinary	☐	Professional	☐
Kinky	☐	Romantic	☐
Hunky	☐		
Sexually dominant	☐	Anything else?	☐
Sexually submissive	☐	_____	

5.6 Is there one particular setting or subject matter that your ideal erotic novel would contain?

_____

SECTION SIX: LAST WORDS

6.1 What do you like best about Black Lace books?

_____

6.2 What do you most dislike about Black Lace books?

_____

6.3 In what way, if any, would you like to change Black Lace covers?

_____

6.4   Here's a space for any other comments:

_____
_____
_____
_____

Thank you for completing this questionnaire. Now tear it out of the book – carefully! – put it in an envelope and send it to:

> **Black Lace**
> **FREEPOST**
> **London**
> **W10 5BR**

No stamp is required if you are resident in the U.K.